I0538267

Sheridan Andorran would never be considered a good man—not even a decent one. He's done far too many questionable things in the name of self-preservation. When his brother orders him to kidnap his niece, Sheridan intends to do it. Except, outside the home where Kendra is staying, he runs across a man charged with stopping him—Rory MacDougal—and the man awakens every hidden desire he's ever felt. One kiss from Rory and Sheridan knows he'll never be able to hide his desires from his homophobic brother again. He does the only thing he can think of to save his own skin. Sheridan flees. A day later, stranded on the side of the road, he starts hitchhiking . . . only to be picked up by Rory. Sheridan learns his brother is dead, his sister is in jail, and the only family he has left—his niece and her father—want nothing to do with him. Rory asks Sheridan to stay. Can he learn how to become a different person, a better man, and make amends to those he owes before his checkered past catches up with him?

Reader Advisory: This story is best read after finishing The Crystal Connoisseur.

The unauthorized reproduction or distribution of this copyrighted work is illegal. Criminal copyright infringement, including infringement without monetary gain, is investigated by the FBI and is punishable by up to 5 years in federal prison and a fine of $250,000.

This book is a work of fiction. Names, characters, places, and incidents either are products of the author's imagination or are used fictitiously. Any resemblance to actual events or locales or persons, living or dead, is entirely coincidental.

Sheridan's Redemption
Copyright © 2020 Charlie Richards
ISBN: 978-1-4874-2866-2
Cover art by Angela Waters

All rights reserved. Except for use in any review, the reproduction or utilization of this work in whole or in part in any form by any electronic, mechanical or other means, now known or hereafter invented, is forbidden without the written permission of the publisher.

Published by eXtasy Books Inc or
Devine Destinies, an imprint of eXtasy Books Inc

Look for us online at:
www.eXtasybooks.com or www.devinedestinies.com

SHERIDAN'S REDEMPTION
WOLVES OF STONE RIDGE: BOOK FIFTY-ONE

BY

CHARLIE RICHARDS

DEDICATION

Family, like branches on a tree, we all grow in different directions
yet our roots remain as one.
~Unknown

CHAPTER ONE

Sheridan Andorran gripped the steering wheel tightly and bowed his head. A low groan of frustration escaped his mouth. Closing his eyes, he bounced his forehead off the top of the wheel a couple of times before resting it there.

Could life get any shittier?

Even as the thought flitted through Sheridan's mind, he cringed. He knew better than to tempt Fate. With the way his life was going, it could.

Since he knew nothing about vehicles, Sheridan didn't even bother popping the hood on the old truck. He wouldn't know what he was looking at anyway. His brother was the one who fixed their vehicles.

Sheridan glanced around, a bout of nerves bursting through him. Even though he knew just thinking about the man—Spencer Andorran—wouldn't make him appear, the hairs on his nape still stood on end. He needed to get moving, so he could stay ahead of the man.

I know he'll come after me. He did before.

After grabbing his backpack from where it rested next to him on the bench seat, Sheridan shoved out of the truck. He pocketed his keys, then slammed the door. Sheridan didn't bother to lock it. The truck was an old piece of shit.

If someone wants to steal it, more power to 'em.

With that thought in mind, Sheridan started walking. He trudged along, putting one foot in front of the other. Pulling his coat tight around him, he shivered against the cold.

Winter in Colorado sucks.

Maybe I'll move to Florida. No one will know me there.

While the winter air chilled his neck, Sheridan said a silent thank you to the universe that the heavy snow from the prior evening had stopped. Even with the heavy-duty tires on the pick-up, he'd still slid around a little. He knew he should have waited for a break in the storm, but he'd needed to get away before Spencer finished with his plan to kick Wilson's ass and came after him, too.

Sheridan had failed in Spencer's order to kidnap their niece, Kendra, Wilson's daughter. Wilson was married to their younger sister, Shandell. Spencer planned to use keeping Kendra away from Wilson as leverage to keep Wilson from divorcing Shandell, stopping their free money flow.

While Sheridan had intended to do as his brother ordered — take Kendra away from the home of where she'd been spending the night at her friend's home — he'd run into an unexpected problem.

Rory MacDougal.

Sheridan felt his body flush hot just thinking about the sexy man. Swallowing hard, he reached down and adjusted his growing prick behind his fly. Shaking his head, he tried not to dwell on their brief meeting.

Recalling that kiss, however, sure made it tough.

Ever since Sheridan realized he was gay at the age of fourteen, he'd had to hide it. His family were bigoted and mean about it. Even after their parents had died, Spencer had kept up the derogatory slurs and name-calling, and Shandell had parroted him.

Sheridan had known he could never allow his older brother and younger sister to find out. To that end, he'd shunned most other interaction besides what was required for his work at the diner. Fortunately, as the cook, he didn't have to do more than talk about orders.

Hearing the rumble of a car engine, Sheridan lifted his head. He saw that it was coming from in front of him, so he ignored it. Instead, he read the road sign he was walking to-ward.

Denver – eight-six miles.

Ugh!

Sighing, Sheridan kept walking.

When another rumble registered, Sheridan realized it was coming from behind him. He stuck out his thumb as he kept moving. Too bad the *Jeep* didn't stop.

Sheridan grimaced as the vehicle driving past him splashed wet spray onto his pants.

Jackass.

Of course, Sheridan knew he didn't have any room to talk. He followed along with all of Spencer's plans. It was easier that way.

Absently rubbing his ribcage, Sheridan recalled Spencer's last *reminder* of his place.

Sheridan had secretly saved up a little over a thousand bucks. It had taken him over a year since he had to squirrel away a few bucks here and there from the cash Spencer gave him to buy beer. Most of the time, Spencer would ask for the change back, but not always.

Once Sheridan had that little nest egg, he had packed a bag, climbed into his pick-up, and driven away. He should have left his phone behind. His brother had tracked him down three towns over.

Spencer had beat the shit out of him. After warning him that trying to walk away from his family obligations would get a broken bone next time, he'd ordered Sheridan home. His brother had followed behind him in his nicer, newer truck, practically on his bumper, all the way home.

Then Spencer had taken his money and had kept careful tabs on his activities. He'd also stepped up his rants on the importance of family and sticking together.

Family values. Ha!

For some reason, sticking together only applied to the three of them. Shandell's husband wasn't family. Neither was Kendra, and when she came to the house with her mother, Sheridan did his best to keep her occupied and away from them both.

The sound of another engine drew Sheridan from his bitter thoughts. He turned and spotted an older *Bronco* approaching. Sticking out his thumb, he tried not to get his hopes up too high.

The vehicle slowed as it approached him, and Sheridan's heart thundered in his chest.

Maybe I won't have to walk the whole way.

To Sheridan's relief, the vehicle pulled onto the shoulder about thirty feet in front of him. He picked up his pace as the driver's side door opened. When the guy exited and turned to face him, Sheridan froze as he stared at the last man he'd ever thought to see again.

"Oh fuck," Sheridan whispered.

Rory MacDougal stalked toward him.

Sheridan's mouth went dry as he took in the man's broad shoulders and strong frame. The well-defined muscles of his legs were showcased in his form-fitting jeans. Even the bulky winter jacket did nothing to hide how fit he was.

Spotting the hungry gleam in Rory's green eyes, Sheridan took a step backward. He saw the man smile, drawing his focus to his mouth. Recalling how those lips felt against his own, he felt his breath catch in his chest.

The memory he'd been fighting all night flashed through his mind.

Sheridan pulled his old truck to a stop at the end of the driveway. Pushing the door open, he slid out . . . right onto a patch of ice. His foot slipped out from under him, and he pinwheeled his arms as he struggled to regain his balance.

Feeling himself falling, Sheridan made a wild grab for the

side of his pick-up bed. He got a hand on it, but the snow running along the top caused his fingers to skate right off again. With a cry, he tucked his arm against his body, preparing to meet the ground.

Except, then he didn't.

Sheridan felt a thick arm around his waist, stopping his momentum. With a tug, whoever had grabbed him easily brought him back upright. He found himself back on his feet, facing the side of his truck.

Whoever held him didn't let him go. Instead, the stranger tightened his hold. He flushed his front to Sheridan's backside, and Sheridan felt the unmistakable touch of cool lips against his neck.

Sheridan gasped upon feeling the brazen move. Confusion swirled through him. He knew he should yank away, but he couldn't seem to convince his feet to move.

"You okay there, handsome?" the man asked in a lightly accented melodious tenor. "Found yer feet?"

Another kiss and nibble along the side of his neck yanked Sheridan from his shocked stupor. He cleared his throat as he took a step forward. At the same time, he pivoted.

While the stranger's arm loosened enough for Sheridan to put a little space between them, he didn't release him. Instead, he settled his hand on Sheridan's hip. He even lifted his other hand and threaded it through his short, dirty-blond hair and cradled his nape.

"Sheridan, isn't it?"

Snapping his focus from the leather-jacket-covered broad shoulders, Sheridan swept his gaze over the stranger's face. He peered into deep green eyes that somehow managed to glimmer in the dim evening light. A bit of scruff bracketed the slightly smiling lips, and his black hair was pulled back from his face.

"You know me?"

The stranger's lips widened as he nodded once. "Got a picture of ye from Wilson," he told him. "He figured ye'd show up here tonight." The man jerked his chin toward the home where his niece was spending the night. "We didn't want ye taking Kendra to use as leverage against him while he's presenting the divorce paperwork to yer sister." Massaging Sheridan's nape, he rumbled, "Now I'm damn glad it was me hangin' around out here."

"You know about that?" Sheridan shook his head as he attempted to step back once more, but the dark-haired stranger moved with him. Seeing as he already knew the answer to that question, Sheridan quickly continued, "Why are you glad? Who are you?" He frowned as he found himself pinned against the side of his truck. "What are you doing?"

"M'name's Rory MacDougal," he told him. "And I'm glad I'm here because ye're goin' to be awfully important to me very soon." His voice turned husky as he dipped his head, his face drawing closer. "And I'm gonna kiss ye."

Before Sheridan could process even half of that, Rory did exactly as he claimed. He pressed their lips together. When he parted his lips and swiped his tongue against Sheridan's bottom one, he let out a soft gasp of surprise.

Rory took complete advantage, thrusting his tongue into Sheridan's mouth. He expertly lapped along Sheridan's appendage, teasing and tasting. His masculine flavor exploded across Sheridan's taste buds, delicious and earthy.

With a whimper of shock, Sheridan felt his blood heat in his veins. His head swam as the kiss continued. His cock thickened, filling out the crotch of his worn jeans.

Upon feeling Rory press his own body against Sheridan's, revealing he had an answering bulge behind his own fly, Sheridan groaned and bucked. He grabbed Rory's jacket and clung. His body undulated against the bigger man's as trembles worked through him.

"Rory? What the fuck, bro?"

A deep, also slightly accented voice, cut through the night air directly to his left.

Lifting his head, breaking the kiss, Rory turned his attention to the speaker. His lips were curved into a wide grin as he stated, "He's my mate, Cullen."

"Fuck a duck," the other man—Cullen—replied, a look of shock etching on his features. "Seriously?"

"Mmm-hmmm." Rory returned his focus to Sheridan. "Oh, yeah."

Swallowing hard, Sheridan read the heat and desire in the man's dark eyes. His features were flushed, and hunger filled his expression. He continued to press his body against Sheridan's, even though Sheridan had managed to stop rutting against the man.

"Well, damn." Cullen cocked his head as he furrowed his eyebrows. "Uh, congrats?"

"Thanks," Rory replied, smiling at Sheridan.

"This is gonna cause a problem or two, Ror," Cullen continued in warning, which drew Rory's gaze back to the other man. "I mean"—he pointed at Sheridan—"he's known for roughing up our brother's mate, *and* he was going to kidnap Kendra." Cullen crossed his arms over his chest. "I mean, ye're a cop, Ror. And sure he's yer mate, but how are ye okay with that?"

Rory frowned at Cullen. "I didn't say that I was okay with his actions, but he's my mate." A muscle in his jaw flexed as he rumbled, "I'll be by his side as he pays restitution and earns his redemption."

"Okay," Cullen replied. Then patted him on the shoulder. "Ye know I got yer back."

"Thanks."

Sheridan's confusion only grew as the pair talked about him like he wasn't there. That was okay because his own mind was going a mile a minute. He realized several things at once.

First — Rory and Cullen must have talked to Wilson about his actions. Two — his brother-in-law was leaving his sister to be with another of their brothers. Three — Rory was a cop.

Holy fuck! He's a cop! If he finds out any of the things I had to help Spencer with, I'm gonna end up in jail.

Sheridan didn't think even Shandell knew, but Spencer had badass breaking and entering skills. He'd helped his brother loot more than one home. Even on the heists where he didn't go in the home, Sheridan drove the getaway car.

While Rory had been chatting with Cullen, his grip on Sheridan had eased. Taking advantage of the man's distraction, he lunged to the right. Clearly surprised, Rory let him go.

Hopping into his truck, Sheridan slammed the door. He ignored Rory's shouted order to stop and started his truck. Seeing Rory reach for his door's handle, Sheridan slapped the lock on top of the door.

Then Sheridan roared away.

Sheridan reached home in record time just as the snow began to fall. Skidding to a stop, he slammed his shifter into park. Without cutting the engine, he raced into the house, using the spare key hidden in a hole beneath the porch railing.

After shooting a text to Spencer, Sheridan quickly filled a backpack. He ignored the chime of his phone. There wasn't anything else for him to say to his brother. He'd already explained that a cop had been waiting outside the home where Kendra was spending the night and that he'd been spotted by the man. Sheridan had even taken a chance and told Spencer that he was running.

Well, I didn't tell him that I'd just received the best damn kiss of my life.

"Come with me, Sheridan," Rory ordered, his soft urging accented voice drawing Sheridan back to the present.

Sheridan glanced around frantically, but there was nowhere to go and no one around.

"Sheridan," Rory crooned, stopping before him. He reached out slowly, as if attempting to soothe a frightened animal. "Ye're okay, my sweet," he purred, resting his hands on Sheridan's shoulders. As Rory gently massaged him, he added, "Ye're safe with me."

"You don't know what you're talking about," Sheridan countered. Even as he shook his head, a tremble of desire trickled down his spine, caused by the way Rory slid his hands higher and caressed the sides of his neck with his thumbs. He would forever blame his next words on the surge of arousal sending his blood out of his brain and straight to his little head. "You don't know me or what I've done."

Rory nodded slowly as he eased even closer. "Ye're right," he agreed, sliding one hand into Sheridan's hair as he cradled his neck with the other. "I do know this, though."

When Rory dipped his head, Sheridan thought he would kiss him again . . . and shame flooded him that he wanted that so damn bad.

Instead, Rory pressed his cheek to Sheridan's own and whispered into his ear, "I'll be at yer side as we get it sorted, my sweet."

Sheridan jerked his head back and stared up into Rory's face, taking in his confident expression.

"You won't feel that way after listening to me talk for ten minutes," Sheridan whispered. Upon seeing the way Rory narrowed his eyes, he continued, "And my brother will never allow us to be together."

CHAPTER TWO

R ory peered into Sheridan's eyes, hating the fear, confusion, and uncertainty he saw swimming within their hazel depths. Chasing his fleeing mate had been a unique kind of torture. Especially after experiencing the most exquisite few moments of his life—feeling his lean, hard body pressed against his own while smelling the heady scent of his arousal perfuming the air.

Will what I have to share next send him running again? Doesn't matter. I'll chase my mate to the ends of the earth and back again.

As a shifter, Rory considered finding his mate the greatest moment of his life. He sure hadn't expected it to be where, when, and with whom. What Cullen had said was true—his youngest brother—Brennan—would have a hard time accepting Sheridan.

I'll make it work. Fate doesn't make mistakes.

Hell, even I can see my mate needs me. Probably even needed me before this.

"I don't know how ye'll take this news," Rory began slowly as he continued to massage Sheridan's neck. "But Spencer will never cause trouble for ye again." Cocking his head, he took in the questioning look that took over Sheridan's features. "Ye're brother is dead. Killed by an associate of mine when he went after Wilson and my youngest brother, Brennan."

Sheridan swallowed so hard his Adam's apple bobbed. His jaw worked, and his face flushed. A tremble even worked through his body.

"Sp-Spencer is dead?" Sheridan whispered.

Rory nodded once. "I'm afraid so."

For nearly a full minute, Sheridan blinked as a myriad of emotions flitted across his features. The scents of confusion, disbelief, and even relief filled the air. Finally, Sheridan cleared his throat. After one more blink, he focused on Rory.

"Your brother said you're a cop."

That hadn't been the response Rory expected, but he nodded anyway. "I am. Out of Stone Ridge."

Sheridan's brows furrowed. "Is that associate you spoke of a cop, too?"

Rory shook his head as a smile toyed at the corners of his lips. "No." He chuckled as he thought of Castrose and cop in the same sentence. "Castrose is a sniper and assassin."

Gaping, Sheridan stared at him with wide eyes.

For a couple of heartbeats, Rory had to fight back his urge to dip his head, seal his lips over Sheridan's, and swirl his tongue deep. He wanted to taste his mate again so fucking badly. Only the knowledge that he didn't know how Sheridan would respond—and he had so much more to explain—helped him keep control.

As Rory had been following the instructions of Raul Braga—a tech-savvy pack-member who'd hacked traffic cameras so he could tell Rory where his mate was, he'd finally understood why Brennan had begun acting so out of character. His youngest brother wasn't normally a reckless man. Unfortunately, finding a mate who was already married had sent his poor youngest brother a little over the edge.

Damn idiot should have come to his family for support and help.

That time was passed, however. Brennan was now happily mated with Wilson. It had all worked out . . . for them.

Now I gotta make it work out for me.

"A-Are you, um—"

Sheridan growing tense wasn't what Rory wanted as he

11

continued to pet his mate's neck. "Am I what, sweet Sheridan?" He smiled at the man he hoped to soon make his lover. "You may ask me anything."

After another hard swallow, with a deep blush staining his cheeks, Sheridan muttered, "Are you a dirty cop?"

Straightening his shoulders, Rory frowned. He opened his mouth, then bit back his initial response of *Why the fuck would ye think that?* Instead, he thought swiftly about their conversation. *Lightbulb!* Rory chuckled. "Ah, because Castrose is an assassin?" As he watched Sheridan nod, he shook his head. "No, I'm not a dirty cop." Deciding to start out as he meant to go, he shared the truth. "While Castrose might have done a few underhanded things in the past, he's a part of our pack now, and he uses his skills to aid our people."

"Pack?"

Rory decided that explanation could wait, so he just nodded. "Anyway, did ye know Shandell set her house on fire out of spite?"

The way Sheridan's lips parted and his eyes widened was answer enough. Still, he shook his head. Then a shiver went through the human as a breeze hit them, and he hunched his shoulders.

Sighing, Rory released Sheridan's neck. He immediately turned and wrapped one arm around his mate's waist. Using his new hold, he guided Sheridan toward the passenger side of his *Bronco.*

"So, that being said, Shandell is cooling her heels in jail," Rory told him as he opened his vehicle's door. "There's nothing and no one to stand in the way of me and you having a relationship."

"Me and you?" Sheridan climbed inside the cabin as he softly repeated the words. Once seated, he frowned at Rory. "Why would a cop be interested in a two-bit crook like me? I could end up in jail. Then how would that look for you?"

Rory growled softly even as he reached in and buckled Sheridan's seatbelt. He couldn't help but notice that even though Sheridan was voicing concerns, he wasn't denying him. That was a start.

"And what's a pack?" Sheridan asked again. "You didn't answer. Is it like a gang?" Hunching a little, he swung his backpack off and set it at his feet. "Spencer is really dead."

Knowing his mate was beyond overwhelmed, Rory leaned in and pressed a kiss to his temple. "I'll take ye home and have a buddy tow yer truck." Then he closed the door and jogged around the hood.

After climbing inside, Rory checked his mirrors, confirming it was safe to return to the road. He turned his *Bronco* around and started them back toward Colin City. Needing to touch, he reached out and rested his hand on Sheridan's knee.

While Rory felt Sheridan tense a little beneath his palm, he didn't try to pull away. He counted that a small victory. His mate might have run, but now he realized it was for different reasons than what Rory had originally thought—for safety from his family.

"Do ye have any idea what's wrong with yer truck?" Rory asked as he squeezed Sheridan's knee. "Run out of gas, maybe?"

Sheridan blinked, then turned his head to look in his direction. "It's not out of gas, and I have no idea." He shrugged. "Spencer was the one who kept it running. He didn't want to buy a new truck for me."

Rory grunted. After squeezing his knee once more, he pulled his phone out of his pocket. "Do ye like yer truck?" he asked curiously as he woke the device.

"It's the only thing in my name," Sheridan murmured, his tone soft, almost vacant-sounding, telling Rory that his mate was about to shut down. "So, yeah. It's pretty important, I guess."

Nodding, Rory scrolled to Kade's name in his contacts and hit the call button.

"Hey, Rory," Kade greeted after a couple of rings. "You find your mate, okay?"

Rory smiled. As a pack enforcer, Kade knew just about everything that went on with their members. "I did," he confirmed, glancing Sheridan's way. His mate stared out the window, his head resting against the backrest. "His truck broke down. Not certain what's wrong with it. Can you or one of yer employees come give it a tow?"

Kade also owned a mechanic's shop in Stone Ridge.

"Sure can," Kade replied. "How's your man taking learning about shifters?"

"I haven't tried to explain that, yet," Rory admitted. "I figured he needed a little time to absorb the facts about his brother and sister."

"Ah, gotcha. So where's the truck, and where do you want it hauled to?"

Rory glanced Sheridan's way again and noticed his eyes were closed. Telling Kade where the truck was located was simple enough. After a quick thought, he asked the enforcer to take Sheridan's ride to his shop to be given a thorough inspection.

"I can do that," Kade confirmed. "I'll head out with the flatbed in ten." After a second of hesitation, he told him, "Best give Alpha Declan a call. He wants to meet your mate at Sheridan's home."

Blowing out a breath, Rory nodded. He knew Kade couldn't see it, so he said, "Will do, Kade."

"Oh, and congratulations, Rory," Kade offered with warmth in his tone. "I know the situation ain't the best, but finding a mate is always a blessing."

"That it is."

Then Kade disconnected the call, and Rory contacted Alpha Declan. He gave the alpha wolf an ETA of when they would make it back to Sheridan's place in Colin City. It should be approximately six hours, seeing as Sheridan had been driving all night, but it had been slow going in the snow. Following him had been dangerous, but Rory had refused to wait until the storm passed.

Rory just felt grateful his mate was safe and with him.

Once Rory had finished chatting with his alpha, pleased to be offered congratulations from the man, he knew he had one more call to make. He glanced Sheridan's way once more, relieved to see his mate had drifted off to sleep. While it probably had more to do with fatigue, stress, and being completely overwhelmed, Rory couldn't help but feel gratitude that Sheridan let down his guard enough to allow sleep to take him.

Pulling up Brennan's contact, Rory called his brother. "Did ye find him?"

"I did," Rory confirmed, not surprised he didn't receive a greeting. "He's safe." After peeking at his mate again, he muttered, "He looks a little undernourished to me, actually."

While Rory had only ever seen Sheridan in a thick winter coat, that was what it felt like the several times he'd held the human in his arms. Just thinking about holding him caused his blood to flow south. His prick plumped behind the fly of his jeans, and he shifted in his seat, trying to find a more comfortable position.

"I'm glad ye found yer mate, Rory," Brennan told him, sounding sincere. Then his deep sigh drifted through the line. "Wish it were someone other than a guy who abused my own mate, but I'll just have to trust Fate knows what she's doin'."

Rory winced. "I know it'll be a bit awkward for a while," he acknowledged. "Still, he's mine." After hearing Brennan grunt, Rory cleared his throat and asked, "Did ye talk to Wilson about restitution?"

"I explained it to him," Brennan confirmed. "My sweet, kind-hearted mate doesn't like the idea of hurtin' anyone . . . even someone who hit him."

Grimacing, Rory looked toward Sheridan once again. From the short interactions he'd had with his mate, he couldn't see how he was a violent person. The man's kiss had been wonderful, if inexperienced, and the way he responded was beyond anything Rory had ever dreamed of.

If Sheridan was gonna respond with his fists, it woulda been when I kissed him.

"It just doesn't fit," Rory muttered, scowling at the snow-covered road. "And he talked about possibly bein' sent to jail."

"Jail?" Brennan growled softly. "He's a criminal, too?"

Rory curled his lip, biting back a snarl of his own only because he didn't want to risk waking Sheridan. "No, I did *not* say that." In truth, Rory thought his mate had alluded to it, but he wasn't going to tell anyone but his alpha that. Before Brennan could press the issue, he stated, "So Wilson didn't give ye any idea what he may want as restitution?" Recalling his brother's comment about inflicting pain, Rory quickly added, "And ye did explain that restitution could be monetary, right?"

Brennan scoffed. "Of course, I told Wilson." Huffing an irritated noise, he added, "And he pretty much just wants Sheridan to leave him and Kendra alone."

"That'll be difficult, considering family and pack gatherings," Rory grumbled.

"I told him the same thing," Brennan admitted on a sigh. "He's still thinkin'."

Rory nodded absently. "With Spencer out of the picture, maybe an apology and heart to heart talk would suffice?"

"Maybe."

Brennan remained silent for a moment, giving Rory enough time to open and close his mouth . . . twice. He just didn't know what to tell his baby brother. Everyone in the MacDougal family had always been close, supportive, and finding mates that had a strained history created tension between all of them.

"At least, Kendra called Sheridan the nice uncle," Brennan offered. "That's somethin'. Right?"

"I bet there's a few stories there. I just don't know if I want to hear them."

Kendra was a sweet seven-year-old daughter. Rory had met her at his niece, Tessa's, sixth birthday party a few weeks prior. The pack had rented out the bowling alley.

When Cullen's son, Chance, had accidentally shifted, Wilson and Kendra had learned of the paranormal world. They'd taken it well, fortunately. Rory had even shifted to his wolf form, allowing Kendra and her friend, Sierra, to pet him.

"Well, I better get off the line," Rory stated. "I am driving, after all."

"Safe travels, brother."

"Thanks."

Rory hung up the line, then placed his phone in a cup holder. Concentrating on the road, he did his best to ignore the magnificent scent of his mate filling the cabin of his *Bronco*. He tightened his hold on the wheel and focused on getting them back to Colin City as swiftly as possible.

In just over five and a half hours, Rory pulled his *Bronco* into the driveway of Sheridan's home. His mate had slept the whole way. He felt a bit loath to wake him, but seeing as he saw Alpha Declan's SUV coming down the street toward the house, he knew he needed to.

Rory reached over and rested his hand on Sheridan's shoulder. Ever-so-gently, he jostled the man. As his mate's beautiful hazel eyes slowly blinked open, Rory smiled at the man.

"We made it, Sheridan," Rory told him softly. "How are ye feeling?"

"Like I gotta piss." Sheridan grimaced, peering at him side-eyed. His cheeks took on a pinkish hue as he muttered, "Sorry."

Chuckling, Rory took off his seatbelt. "Then let's head inside."

Sheridan nodded as he took off his own belt.

As Rory followed Sheridan into the house, he knew it was time for some hard truths.

God, I hope he's in a decent frame of mind to accept.

CHAPTER THREE

Sheridan led the way into the house, his brain feeling like it was still in a sleep-haze. Pausing in the foyer, he placed his backpack on the floor. Then he sat on the boot box and removed his footwear.

Once done, he rested there with his hands on his thighs. He stared vacantly across the room. The foyer opened into a front living space — what their mother used to call the sitting room or salon.

They'd rarely used it.

To his left, he could see the dining room and the edge of the kitchen bar on the right. There was a family room to the left of the dining area. After their parents had passed, Spencer had surround sound installed, and he'd replaced the old sofa with a massive reclining one that had a cooler in the middle.

Sheridan tried to remember how many beer cans had been left stacked on the end table next to where Spencer always sat.

Why do I care? I'm not entertaining Rory.

I still want to impress him.

While Sheridan didn't know why that was the case, it still was.

"Are ye okay?" Rory placed his hand on Sheridan's shoulder and squeezed lightly. "Can I get ye a glass of water or maybe something a little stronger?" Then he chuckled softly. "If ye have it here, anyway."

"I think . . ." Sheridan hesitated, frowning. Then he lifted his gaze to Rory. "Why are you being so nice to me? I don't deserve it."

"Fortunately, I don't care what ye think ye deserve." Rory lowered to one knee before him, cradling his jaw with his free hand. "Ye're special to me, Sheridan. All those questions ye had about pack and why I don't care that Castrose is a sniper and assassin? It's all tied together."

Sheridan swallowed hard, seeing the sincerity in Rory's deep green eyes. "Does it have anything to do with why I'm so damn attracted to you?" Realizing what he'd blurted out, he grimaced and lowered his gaze. "I've always been able to hide it in the past. My family wouldn't have approved."

"I know it sounds callous," Rory murmured, his lips pinching. "But I'm glad they're no longer a factor."

"Me, too." Then Sheridan hunched his shoulders and lowered his gaze to the floor. "Are Wilson and Kendra okay? You said Spencer died trying to hurt Wilson, but I forgot to ask."

"They're fine," Rory told him. Then he used his hold on his jaw to urge his face upward. "And it's nice that ye asked."

Rory leaned forward, holding his gaze.

Sheridan felt his heart trip in his chest. He knew what was coming. The man was going to kiss him.

Do I want that?

Hell yes!

Going against Spencer's edicts didn't come easy, though. Sheridan felt his pulse spike, and trepidation surged through his veins. He felt sweat break out on his brow, and his fingers gripped the fabric of his jeans tightly.

"Relax," Rory purred just before his lips touched Sheridan's own. He held Sheridan's gaze as he kept the touch light. Then he lifted his mouth and murmured, "Ye're safe with me, Sheridan."

Then Rory tightened his hold on Sheridan's jaw and sealed their mouths together. He swiped along Sheridan's lower lip, creating delicious tingles to trickle down his neck. Sheridan opened his mouth, recalling the way Rory had plundered him before and wanting to feel that again.

Rory didn't disappoint. He thrust his tongue into Sheridan's mouth and began teasing their appendages together. He mapped Sheridan's teeth and tongue before tipping his head to the side a bit more, pushing the kiss deeper.

Sheridan tried to keep up, but he couldn't. His experience with kissing was exactly nil, zilch, zippo, none. He felt his mind fuzz out as he grabbed Sheridan's jacket and held on for the ride.

The ring of the doorbell pierced Sheridan's senses, and he jolted. The move caused their lips to part, and Rory smiled at him. Even as Sheridan struggled to catch his breath, the other man grinned at him.

"You taste divine," Rory told him, licking his lips. "I'll get that."

Then Rory rose to his feet and turned toward the front door. He took the couple of steps necessary, then opened it.

"Hi, Alpha Declan," Rory greeted the black man on the other side of the door. "Please, come in."

Rory took a step backward, making way for their guests.

Sheridan popped up from the boot box as he watched several people file in behind the black man. Glancing between all the strangers—most of whom were really big, brawny, and had plenty of muscles—he began backing toward the nearby stairs. The hairs on his arms stood on end as he wrapped his arms around himself.

"Hey, easy, Sheridan," Rory rumbled, crossing to him. He wrapped him in his arms and pulled him against his chest. "Ye're safe. Remember?"

Realizing he was trembling and stopping it were two different things. He glanced around at everyone again, then met Rory's gaze. All the big men were damn intimidating, and he bet their fists hurt.

"Hey, you're okay," the little blond man soothed. His smile appeared understanding. "You're among friends."

Rory nodded as he threaded his fingers through Sheridan's short hair and gently massaged his scalp. Even as he soothed Sheridan, he turned his attention to the big black man. "I don't like the way he's respondin', Alpha Declan. There's more going on here than we know."

The black man—Alpha Declan—dipped his head in a nod. "Agreed." He cupped the blond's nape, drawing the man's attention. "Why don't ye head into the kitchen and see if ye can find somethin' to help calm Sheridan's nerves."

Nodding, the blond pursed his lips.

Alpha Declan didn't miss a beat. He bent and pecked a kiss to his lips. Then the blond strode deeper into the house.

"I'll give him a hand," an auburn-haired guy stated, striding after him.

Sheridan gaped. While Alpha Declan had an Irish accent—a little thicker than Rory's family's—the redhead had a different one. While he'd only heard it on TV, Sheridan thought it was Cajun.

That wasn't what intrigued Sheridan, though. "You're gay?" he blurted out, staring at Alpha Declan.

"I am," Alpha Declan replied, a small smile curving his thick lips. He waved at the others. "We all are except him." He pointed at a black-haired man who had a resemblance to Rory.

"Wow!" Sheridan wouldn't have thought it of any of them. They certainly didn't look it. He looked at Rory for confirmation.

Rory nodded once, a smile curving his lips. He pointed at the black guy. "This is our pack's leader, Alpha Declan." Then he indicated a broad-shouldered, fair-skinned man with ice-blue eyes. "Beta Dixon." One by one, he pointed out everyone. "Enforcer Gracen, Enforcer Mishka. Enforcer Manon is the Cajun who accompanied the slender blond, who is Doctor Lark Trystan, the alpha's mate." Finally, he pointed at the black-haired man who looked similar to him. "And this is my eldest brother, Cliff. He's the pack's head tracker."

Nibbling his lower lip, Sheridan peered around at everyone. "Pack. Alpha." He began repeating words that seemed to have significance. "Beta. Enforcer. Tracker." Cocking his head, Sheridan glanced toward the kitchen. "Mate." Then, lifting his chin and focusing on Rory, he asked, "You said you weren't part of a motorcycle gang, so what does all that mean?"

"Why don't we take this into the living room," Lark suggested, appearing from the kitchen. He held a tray in his hand, which Sheridan didn't know where he'd found. "There's a huge comfy-looking sofa."

"And a couple of lounge chairs." Manon held up a garbage bag. "Which I'll unbury from beer cans."

Sheridan felt his cheeks heat as he was guided forward, following the alpha, while a few of the others followed. "Sorry," he muttered, rubbing the back of his neck. "Spencer never picks up after himself."

"Not your fault unless you contributed to the pyramid," Manon stated, indicating the six-tiered tower on the end table.

Evidently, Spencer had run out of room there and begun chucking them onto the nearby chairs.

Shaking his head, Sheridan admitted, "Not much of a beer drinker. I'd sneak an occasional bottle of wine into my room."

"Sneak?" Lark asked as he set the tray down on the newly cleared table. Straightening, he turned to face them. "Why sneak?"

"Uh." Spotting the glass tumblers and bottles of spirits, Sheridan shifted his weight from foot to foot. "Wine isn't a man's drink."

Snorting, Dixon claimed, "I love wine. A good bottle of Riesling with dinner is one of my favorites." Then he grabbed a tumbler as well as the whiskey bottle. "Damn. You *like* this rot-gut?" He scowled at the bottle, setting it back down. "I'll be right back. I have wine in my truck."

"Why do ye have wine in yer truck?" Cliff asked curiously, following him. "Need a hand?"

Dixon shrugged his massive shoulders and stated, "I was grocery shopping when Declan called me." He beckoned, adding, "Sure. I have a few different bottles."

"Nice!" Cliff disappeared behind the bigger man.

"I'll drink it," Mishka stated, grabbing the whiskey.

Grabbing a tumbler, Gracen held it up. "Me, too."

Over the next ten minutes, Dixon and Cliff returned with the wine. They opened a couple of different bottles and poured some into the tumblers. Everyone found a seat—Lark on Declan's lap in one of the recliners.

Sheridan found himself squished between the arm of the sofa and Rory. A glass of white wine had been pressed into his hand by Dixon. While he preferred red, it was a damn sight better than beer or liquor.

"So—" Alpha Declan began after sipping his whiskey. "We're not a biker gang. Do ye believe in the paranormal?"

Almost choking on his sip of wine, Sheridan stared at Declan with wide eyes. He forced his throat to work, allowing him to swallow. Then he managed to parrot, "Paranormal?" His voice squeaked a little, but Sheridan couldn't help it.

Alpha Declan nodded. "Yes. The paranormal."

"D-Do you mean, like, ghosts and spirits and stuff?" Sheridan slowly asked.

"While those *are* out there, no." Dixon took up the conversation. "We mean shifters, vampires, gargoyles." He began flicking up his fingers on one hand as he balanced his wine on the thigh with his other. "Demons. Angels. That kind of shit."

"Nnnoooooo." Sheridan tipped his head to the side. "Why?"

Cliff scoffed softly as he lifted his wine glass in salute.

"Welcome to the rabbit hole, Alice."

Widening his eyes, Sheridan swallowed hard. He glanced around the group. Most of the men wore smirks or smiles. Lark snickered. Rory growled, glaring at Cliff.

Lifting his hand, his palm out, Cliff shrugged. "Sorry, bro."

Lark shook his head. "Okay, so . . . I know this is going to be a little hard to accept, but I promise it's all true." Pausing, he scowled as he met Declan's gaze. "Wow! That sounds like I'm about to share something crazy. Doesn't it?"

"To most humans, what you're about to share *is* crazy," Dixon stated. Then he focused on Sheridan. "We call ourselves a pack because we're wolf shifters. We share our body and mind with a wolf, and we can turn into that animal at will." As Sheridan gaped at him, Dixon waved his hand. "Be aware. We are *not* dangerous in our animal form unless provoked. We can think and reason while a wolf, just like we can in our human form." He indicated his massive frame.

Sheridan turned his attention to Rory. "Y-You believe you can, um"—he hesitated, because saying the words out loud just seemed so ludicrous—"that you can turn into a wolf?"

"Seeing is believing," Rory commented even as he nodded. "Shall I show ye?"

Snorting, Sheridan muttered, "Don't you need the full moon or something?"

Rory shook his head. "No, my sweet mate. A shifter can change form at will." He rocked forward and rose to his feet. Handing his whiskey tumbler to Gracen, who sat next to him, Rory turned and grabbed the hem of his shirt. "Remember, I know exactly who ye are and what ye mean to me. I would never *ever* hurt you."

Sheridan didn't know what to say. While these guys all seemed decent and nice—something he wasn't familiar with—they were beyond crazy. *That* he did have experience with.

His brother had just been a different sort of irrational.

"Okay," Sheridan murmured, nodding slowly. He wouldn't counter a damn thing Rory said. On the rare occasion he'd done that to his brother, he'd gotten a pounding.

Taking a sip of wine, Sheridan waited. He enjoyed the flavor, which surprised him. Perhaps he'd always picked up cheap white when he'd bought it.

Sheridan made a mental note to check the bottle's label.

Then Sheridan's attention was drawn back to Rory . . . because the man was getting naked. A twist of jealousy churned in his gut, and he scowled. After a glance around at the other men, who didn't seem in the least bit surprised by Rory getting nude—although Lark was staring into his wine glass—Sheridan couldn't help himself.

"What the hell are you doing?" Sheridan snapped.

Rory smiled at him while he was unbuttoning and unzipping his jeans. "I know ye don't believe me, yet, but I really do turn into a wolf, Sheridan." He shoved down his jeans as he crouched on the ground. "I don't want to ruin my clothes when I shift."

"I—" Sheridan began. Then he snapped his mouth shut. "Holy shit, I'm jealous." Whispering the words, he glared at the floor. "Why the fuck—"

"That's normal for mates," Gracen told him softly, having obviously heard him. "We don't like anyone seeing our partners naked, either, but with a shifter, there is a certain degree of nudity that you have to get used to."

Sheridan had no idea how to respond to that. Meeting the other man's gaze, he tried to see the crazy within the depths of his brown eyes. Except, there was none.

The dark-haired guy's expression was calm, relaxed, and serene. He truly believed what he was spouting off.

"What's a mate?"

Gracen smiled. "You are Rory's mate," he told him. "The

other half of his soul. The man he will share the rest of his several hundred-years-long life with."

"We're seriously doing this out of order," Dixon muttered before knocking back the rest of his wine.

As Dixon reached for the bottle to refill it, Sheridan opened his mouth to question the pair. Except, the sound of snapping and popping caught his attention. He focused on Rory . . . and gaped.

Rory's body was . . . changing. His legs and arms shortened. A tail emerged from his body, and fur sprouted on his skin. His face elongated, ears grew, and sharp teeth extended from his gums.

"Oh my god," Sheridan whispered, his heart skittering in his chest. "It's real."

Then his eyes rolled to the back of his head, and he slumped.

CHAPTER FOUR

"Catch him," Dixon hollered. "He's goin' down!"

"Shit," Gracen growled.

"We did not prepare him well enough for seeing a shift," Manon claimed.

As Rory finished his shift, he barely made out those comments over the sounds of his form changing. While he knew the sight and noises of a paranormal going from man to animal or back again could be somewhat grotesque, it didn't actually hurt.

Instead, it felt like that first really good stretch after waking from sleep.

Rory opened his eyes and peered at the sofa. He saw Sheridan slumped against the arm. Gracen held his glass of wine, probably having saved it from his mate's now-limp hands. Lark knelt before the man, checking his pulse.

Whining softly, Rory padded over to Sheridan's side. He peered questioningly at the alpha-mate. After a few more seconds, Lark smiled and scratched Rory's furry head.

"He's just sleeping," Lark assured. "I hear he's had a rough couple of days, and he's probably a little overwhelmed." Tapping his temple, he added, "Let's give him fifteen minutes before we wake him."

Nodding his canine head, Rory glanced around the group. All his pack-mates sported understanding expressions. None of them appeared too concerned about Sheridan.

"Go ahead and changed back, Rory," Declan ordered gently. "Ye'll need yer voice when he wakes."

Rory nuzzled his head against Sheridan's leg, then crossed back to his rumpled clothes. He sat on his butt and shifted back again. After half a minute, back in his human form, Rory stood and yanked on his jeans. He'd just finished buttoning them when the trill of a phone caught his attention.

Tipping his head, Rory realized it was coming from upstairs. He knew Alpha Declan had given Raul Spencer's phone—confiscated by Castrose. When Raul had pinged Sheridan's phone after he'd fled, Rory had learned his mate had left it behind.

Curious, Rory hustled up the stairs, following the noise. He spotted the flashing screen on a neatly made bed in the room to the left. Grabbing it, Rory answered.

"Hello?"

"Who is this?" an angry male voice demanded. "Where's Sheridan?"

"Sheridan isn't available right now," Rory replied evenly, not liking the tone of the asshat on the other end of the line. "Can I take a message?"

"Yeah," the man barked. "You can tell that lazy, no-good fucker that he's fired!"

Realizing that the guy had to be Randy Newmann, Sheridan's boss, Rory winced. He hated playing suck-up to the foul-mouthed bastard, but Rory didn't know if Sheridan would want to keep his job now that he could stay in town. Their computer tech had told him that his mate was a cook at a local diner.

Of course, hopefully I'll convince him to move to Stone Ridge soon.

"Please don't do that, sir," Rory urged softly. "Sheridan's brother passed away last night, and his sister went a little crazy. She burned her house down, and now she's in jail." He hoped sharing a bit of Sheridan's woes would appeal to Randy's sense of decency . . . if he had one. "He's lying down right now. I'm sure with all the shocks over the last twenty-four hours, he just forgot to call."

For a moment, Rory didn't get a reply. Only the continued sound of his heavy breathing through the line confirmed the man was still there. Finally, he heard Randy huff in irritation.

"Fine, but he'd better show up tomorrow at six AM for Linda's morning shift," Randy ordered. "I had to call her in to cover Sheridan's shift today."

"I'll let him know," Rory assured.

"Hey, who are you?" Randy asked.

Rory realized he hadn't told the man the first time he'd asked. "My name's Rory MacDougal. I'm a friend of Sheridan's."

Randy's snort came through the line. Just before the man hung up, he muttered, "Didn't think that loser had any friends."

Rolling his eyes, Rory lowered the phone. He spotted several missed calls over the last four hours, as well as a couple of messages. They were all from the same number that he'd just answered.

Rory winced, shaking his head. He bet the man's messages weren't flattering. While he was tempted to delete them all, he resisted.

Peering around the room, Rory took in his mate's personal space. He only felt a niggle of guilt at poking around. After all, he needed to learn more about the man.

The room contained the standard furniture—a bed, a nightstand, and a dresser. There was also a bookshelf. Two shelves contained rows of old paperbacks—mysteries mostly, with a couple of fantasy adventure thrown in. The bottom shelf had a few cookbooks stacked on it.

Rory found the top shelf the most interesting. There were over a dozen small carved animals on it. The whittling knife rested off to the right side as well as a half-finished animal.

"Damn, he's talented."

Opening the closet, Rory saw a tidy space with few clothes. A couple of jackets and long-sleeved flannels hung to one side. The other side contained even more books and whittled animals.

Rory closed the sliding doors and moved to the dresser. Before opening the drawer, he hesitated. "Okay. Maybe that is going too far." Turning away, he headed out of the room.

The second door on the left was open, revealing a bathroom—also neat and tidy. The door across from it was a plain-looking guest room. That left three more doors—one ended up being a linen closet.

Figuring the double doors at the end of the hallway was the master suite—and Spencer's—he saved that room for last. Instead, he gripped the knob to the second door on the right. To his surprise, it was locked.

Expecting it to be an office, he easily used his shifter strength to break the lock and open the door.

Rory whistled under his breath.

While the room was definitely a workspace, it wasn't an office. Folding tables lined the wall straight ahead and to the right. A cabinet was off to the left, which was closed with a padlock. Black velvet had been spread across most of the table space.

On the table to the right rested a lamp with a moveable arm. There was also a magnifying glass on a stand, also easy to maneuver. A bracelet lay on the black velvet positioned between them as well as a number of intricate tools.

Rory swallowed hard as he drew closer. His heart thudded in his chest as he took in the jewels embedded amidst the gold. He figured something gorgeous was probably in the design of the center, but the bracelet had been flipped over to reveal the back of the band. Leaning down, Rory saw there was an inscription—or a partial one.

Always in my —

The rest of whatever had been engraved there had been

ever-so-carefully scraped away. If he hadn't read the first half, he wouldn't even have known there was once something written there. Standing, he rubbed at his chest as he shook his head.

"What the hell are ye involved with, Sheridan?" Rory could guess, and he didn't like where his guesses were going.

Shaking his head, Rory exited the room. He hesitated only an instant before pushing open the door to the master suite. Wincing, he lifted his hand to his nose as his sinuses were assailed with the smells of booze and body odor—caused by the empty cans and clothes scattered over the floor.

Disgusting.

Rory spotted a similar black cloth stretched across the dresser. Several expensive-looking pieces rested on it—a couple of rings, a necklace, and a pocket watch. Beside the fabric was a digital camera.

Rubbing the back of his neck, Rory heaved a sigh. He would bet his left nut that Sheridan was the one to remove the engraving on the bracelet, considering his whittling skills. No way could a drunken Spencer be that precise.

So my mate is *involved in something illegal. Where does the stolen property come from, though?*

"Hey, Ror!" Cliff called up the stairs. "Ye're mate's waking up."

With a deep sigh, Rory rushed back downstairs. His brother must have seen something in his expression or scent. He rested his hand on his shoulder and squeezed.

"What is it?" Cliff asked softly.

"Something illegal was going on in this house," Rory whispered. Seeing his brother's eyes widen, he shrugged. Then Rory turned his attention to the living room where everyone waited. "The call was from Sheridan's boss, Randy. Guess he missed his shift."

Alpha Declan nodded as he pointed at Sheridan.

Rounding the sofa, Rory saw his mate sitting up. His eyes

were wide in his face, and the scent of nerves rolled off of him. The tension in his shoulders did ease a little when he spotted Rory.

Smiling at him, Rory settled on the sofa beside him, holding out his phone. "I convinced yer boss not to fire ye for not showing up or calling for yer shift." Upon seeing Sheridan's surprised expression, he added, "I wasn't certain if ye'd want to continue working there."

"How'd you manage that?" Sheridan asked in a quiet voice. "Randy's been looking for a reason to fire me for months."

"I told him yer brother passed away and yer sister went a little crazy. I may have implied it was from grief. He said ye have to take Linda's six AM shift tomorrow," Rory added, offering him a smile. Reaching out, he took Sheridan's hand between both of his own. "Why was he trying to fire ye?"

Sheridan's focus fell to their clasped hands, but to Rory's pleasure, he didn't try to pull away.

"He's gay, and Spencer has made some really nasty comments about him." Sheridan shrugged. "So he takes it out on me and gives me the shit shifts."

Humming, Rory nodded. "Well, if ye don't want to work there anymore, ye don't have to. I have more than enough to support ye until ye decide what ye want to do now."

"Why are you trying to help me?" Sheridan asked, glancing around the room. "And why did they all come? I'm not going to attack Wilson or Kendra." His expression turned pained as he quietly added, "I won't even call them if they don't want me to, although I'll miss Kendra." A sad smile flickered at the corners of his lips. "She's such a good kid."

"She *is* a good kid," Rory agreed. Lifting Sheridan's hand to his lips, he pressed a kiss to his knuckles. "Ye remember what I did before ye"—he cleared his throat and winked—"fainted?"

Sheridan's cheeks pinked.

Leaning closer, Rory whispered, "That's a pretty look on you. I'd love to see how far yer blush goes down yer body."

Then Rory pressed a kiss to Sheridan's cheek, enjoying the slight rasp of his very light five o'clock shadow. Guessing that Sheridan hadn't shaved in days, Rory figured his mate probably wouldn't be able to grow much of a beard. That was okay. Rory liked the way Sheridan looked as is.

Clearing his throat, Sheridan muttered, "Y-Yeah. Um, you turned into . . . something else." A shudder passed through his body. "How is, how is that possible?"

Rory released Sheridan's hand with his right one so he could wrap that arm around his mate. "Paranormals live and work right alongside humans, my sweet mate. We always have." Massaging Sheridan's hand lightly, Rory told him, "We hide in plain sight because we know the dangers of prejudice. Over the course of history, just about every group has been discriminated against at some point." Grimacing, he added, "Hell, many still are even today."

Sheridan nodded slowly as his eyebrows furrowed. "Okay. So." Then he paused. "But why tell me?"

"Every paranormal has a mate out there," Dixon cut in, relaxing in his chair. "That person is the other half of the shifter's soul. A special person that the paranormal can bond with and spend their long life with." The big, fair-featured man tipped his wine glass in Sheridan's direction. "That's you, Sheridan. You are Rory's mate. After you bond with him, your life will extend to match Rory's, and you'll have hot sex daily."

"Sometimes several times a day," Manon added.

"And it's not just hot, it's *super* hot. Lava hot." Lark grinned and waggled his eyebrows.

Declan chuckled as he pressed a kiss to the side of Lark's neck.

"Plus, Rory will be devoted to you," Cliff told him from where he currently leaned against a nearby wall. His right foot was crossed over his left, and he stared at Sheridan with a solemn gaze. "My brother will never stray and will always have yer best interests at heart. Yer happiness will be his happiness." Then Cliff's eyes narrowed, "So if ye're involved in some shady shit, it's time we know now, so we can help get ye out of it."

Rory grimaced as he watched the blood drain from Sheridan's face. "I was going to ease into that, Cliff," he said with a growl.

"You saw the room," Sheridan mumbled. "Didn't you?"

"I did," Rory confirmed. "I went upstairs to get yer phone when it started ringing." Shrugging, he admitted, "I was curious and snooped a bit."

Even as Sheridan's face darkened once more, he muttered, "Spencer normally keeps that room locked. I wonder —"

"I broke the lock," Rory told him, squeezing his hand lightly. "A paranormal has increased strength and speed. We are immune to human diseases, and our bones are tougher. We also heal faster." Teasing his fingertips up and down Sheridan's spine, Rory explained, "And some of those attributes will pass on to you once we bond."

Just talking about bonding caused his cock to twitch. He wanted to sink into his mate so damn bad. His scent was driving him to distraction, and he couldn't help but press his nose close to his neck and breathe him in.

Fresh air, male musk, and something earthy, something all Sheridan's own.

Yum!

"Focus, Rory," Declan ordered, although his tone sounded teasing. Then his attention turned to Sheridan. "Rory is a member of my pack. As ye are his mate, that means you will be, too." His eyes narrowed. "I don't tolerate abuse in my pack . . . or crime." Declan pointed toward the ceiling. "What has been going on here, Sheridan? Who was the criminal? You or yer brother?"

A tremble worked through Sheridan's body. His grip on Rory's hand tightened, and he pressed closer against him. Rory didn't think Sheridan even knew he did it, but pride filled him that his mate took comfort from him.

Just when Sheridan opened his mouth to respond, a phone trilled, breaking the silence.

Declan held up his hand, then pulled out his phone. "Raul," he said by way of greeting.

With his shifter hearing, Rory had no trouble hearing the human through the line.

"Hey, Alpha. Sorry to interrupt, but a call came in to Spencer's phone from a guy listed as Hook-up." Raul chuckled before saying, "At first I thought it'd be some chick he occasionally bangs. But it wasn't." His tone sobered. "It was a guy saying the money had been wired into Spencer's account, and he should place the goods at the drop tonight. Any idea what he's talking about?"

Declan met Rory's gaze. He arched a brow in question, since he knew every shifter in the room would be able to hear Raul.

"My guess would be stolen jewelry," Rory told his alpha.

Sheridan hunched his shoulders as he nodded in confirmation.

CHAPTER FIVE

Sheridan scrubbed a hand over his face, his mind whirling. *Shit. Shit, shit, shit!*

Payne expected some jewelry, and Sheridan had no idea what Spencer had promised him. Hell, he didn't even know where the drop was. His brother had never shared that information with him.

And when Payne doesn't get his stuff, he's gonna come after me. Oh god!

A shudder worked through Sheridan. He'd met Payne once, and that had been enough. The guy wasn't big like some of these shifters, but he'd been intimidating as hell . . . and mean.

Shifters. So weird.

"Hey," Rory crooned, nuzzling his neck. "Ye're tensing up, my mate. Talk to me." He nipped at Sheridan's flesh. "What's going through that mind of yers?"

"Spencer's hook-up calls himself Payne, and I bet he can dish it out," Sheridan replied, a tremble working through him. He didn't think it was all from fear, either. He'd never been touched the way Rory did now, and his blood was flowing to his cock. "If Payne doesn't get his jewelry, he'll come after us. Um, me," he amended. "Spencer never missed a drop as far as I know."

"Payne," Manon repeated with a snort. "What a douchey name."

Cliff snorted as Dixon grinned broadly. Gracen nodded. While Lark snickered, even Declan's lips twitched.

"Maybe," Sheridan half agreed. "But I wouldn't want to go against him."

"Do ye know what this guy is expecting?" Declan asked, cocking his head. "If ye drop it off to him, we can follow him back to his place and get him arrested."

Sheridan shook his head, nibbling his bottom lip.

Before Sheridan could explain, Rory squeezed his hand and stated, "It really would be the easiest way."

"I wish I could help, but I can't," Sheridan admitted. "Spencer didn't let me in on that side of the business."

"What did you do for him, then?" Dixon asked curiously.

"And where did all the jewelry come from?" Rory pressed a kiss to his neck again before whispering, "Did ye help him steal it?"

"Sometimes. If the house was big enough and he knew they were on vacation," Sheridan admitted, bowing his head. "Mostly, I acted as look-out and drove the get-away car."

Alpha Declan hummed as nodded. "Anything else?"

Bobbing his head a little, Sheridan admitted, "When Spencer discovered I'm really good at wood carving, he started having me scrape off or disfigure any identifying marks on the jewelry he stole." He glanced around before turning his attention back to the floor. "You know, something that someone could use to identify it to a pawnbroker or insurance or something."

"What's your cut in this?" Dixon looked more curious than upset about anything he'd said.

"My cut?" Realizing what Dixon meant, Sheridan waved his hand vacantly. "A roof over my head, food to eat, and clothes on my back."

"So, your brother didn't put some of the money into an account of your own?" Manon leaned forward, staring at him with interest. "Just your paychecks from the diner go in there?"

Sheridan shook his head. "I don't have a bank account of my own. My paychecks go into Spencer's account."

Seeing the men exchange looks, Sheridan could guess at what they thought—he was a total loser for allowing his brother so much control over everything. Sheridan had thought that way enough times, after all.

"Well, at least now the account will pass to you, and you can just wire the money back to Payne." Lark's smile appeared reassuring as he gazed at him. "Right?"

Shaking his head, Sheridan grimaced. "Shandell is the sole heir. Everything goes to her." He rubbed his free hand over his thigh as he saw the confused expressions on the other's faces. Knowing it was lame, Sheridan still offered, "He believed we needed to care for our little sister above all things, because we're the big brothers."

Gracen rubbed the back of his neck as he scowled. "I don't mean to sound like an ass, but why didn't you leave?"

"I tried," Sheridan replied. Sighing, he muttered, "He found me and beat the shit out of me."

A low growl rumbled from Rory. "Well, no one will lay a hand on ye ever again," he snarled.

Instead of the show of aggression causing fear in him, warmth curled in his gut. He almost smiled. Then he realized the man would actually take on his troubles, and he didn't want the man getting hurt because of his family's mess.

"I should really leave town," Sheridan began, glancing around at everyone. "I can't give the money back, and I can't give him the jewelry." Another thought struck, and he frowned. "Well, he knows where we live, so I guess he could come here. Or if you give me Spencer's phone, I could call him and let him know what's going on. Maybe he'll tell me what he paid for and where to put it."

"He won't believe ye," Rory warned, shaking his head. Sheridan gave the man a questioning look, so Rory told him,

"He's a criminal, and he'll think that it's a trick." Frowning, he added slowly, "Most likely, he'd end up going to ground for a while until he feels safe. Then he'll circle back around to come after you."

Declan sighed deeply. "Ye'd constantly be lookin' over yer shoulder." He shook his head. "No, we need a plan to deal with him immediately." Then he curled his lip. "And we need to know if he's connected with any other criminal elements."

"And we should probably return all that jewelry upstairs," Rory commented, shrugging. "Sorry, as a cop, I've seen plenty of emotional distress caused by robberies."

Sheridan cringed, knowing he had helped cause plenty of that over the years.

"Hey, I'm sorry, my mate," Rory rumbled, hugging him close. "I didn't mean to make ye feel guilty."

Shrugging one shoulder, Sheridan mumbled, "It's something I'm used to."

Obviously sensing a subject change was in order, Rory turned and focused on Cliff. "Our family has that small cabin in the mountains. Home territory, and we'll know if a stranger comes to the area."

"I always like home-field advantage," Cliff replied with a wink. He grinned widely as he waggled his brows. "It'll also give ye time to bond with yer mate."

Rory chuckled huskily. "Yep."

Having heard the term a few times, Sheridan furrowed his brows as he focused on Rory. "What does that mean? What's bonding?"

The men around him laughed quietly, grinning widely.

Manon waggled his brows. "A shifter bonds with his mate through sex and a claiming bite, combining their life forces."

"It's very pleasurable," Gracen rumbled, his expression turning a little vacant.

Declan chuckled before explaining, "That way, yer aging

will slow, and he won't outlive ye."

"It also means that if you die, the shifter dies, too," Lark told him, his expression turning serious. "Or vice-versa, so don't go looking for trouble."

Sheridan gaped as he looked at them with wide eyes. "N-No. Never." He focused on Rory. "You want to bond with me? Why? You don't even know me?"

Rory released his hand so he could cradle his jaw. "Ye remember me telling ye that Fate lets us know who our mate is?" Rubbing his thumb along his jawline, Rory smiled at him. "Finding you is a blessing, and we'll get to know each other in time."

Licking his lower lip slowly, Sheridan stared into Rory's deep green eyes. He seemed so confident, comfortable with the idea. The man seemed completely fine with the idea of Fate deciding on who his perfect partner should be.

Am I fine with it?

Sheridan saw the calm confidence in Rory's deep eyes. He read the serenity in his expression. Even every touch Rory had given him had been filled with desire . . . and kindness.

It caused his heart to thud wildly in his chest, and he practically melted from it. Kindness had been in short supply for most of his adult life. These men, these strangers, had offered more of it in one afternoon than Sheridan had experienced in years.

"Okay." Sheridan whispered the word.

Rory's eyes widened for an instant. Then a wide grin curved his lips. "Okay?"

Sheridan nodded. "Yeah."

"Well, okay, then." Rory seemed surprised by his agreement, but pleased, too.

Declan cleared his throat. "There is one other thing we need to discuss."

Sheridan found pulling free of Rory's hand and drawing away from his heated gaze was surprisingly difficult. Arousal simmered in his veins. He really liked the way Rory looked and touched him.

After swallowing hard, Sheridan focused on Declan. Upon seeing the serious expression on the dark man's features, a shiver of unease worked its way down his spine. He shifted uneasily on the sofa cushion.

"Wh-What would that be?"

Had everything really been all too good to be true? Is this where the other shoe drops? What will I have to give up to stay with Rory?

Sheridan didn't have much. Even the house would pass to Shandell, regardless of the fact that she was in jail and would likely be there for twenty-plus years if the first-degree arson charges stuck. She could order him out on the street.

I'll need to move out anyway, considering the threat from Payne.

"I would like to know why ye beat up Wilson," Declan stated. "Several times. Why were ye going to take Kendra away from him?"

Wincing, Sheridan bowed his head. He couldn't hold Declan's gaze. Shame and guilt roared through him, replacing any trace of arousal he'd been feeling.

"Please tell us, Sheridan," Rory urged. "Do ye have aggressive tendencies we need to know about?" He rubbed over his thigh, perhaps trying to soothe him. "Because ye don't seem like the type."

"I'm not," Sheridan mumbled. Recalling his question, he shook his head. "And I don't. It's just —" He forced himself to meet Declan's gaze. To his surprise, he found no condemnation in the man's gray eyes — only concern. "Even though Spencer was shorter than me, he was always stronger." Rubbing the back of his neck, Sheridan continued, "And dominant. A bully. He . . . I . . . I know it doesn't excuse my actions, but it was do as he said or get the shit beat out of me, and —" Sheridan stopped and closed his eyes. "I hated it, but I didn't feel like I had a choice."

"Self-preservation can make us do things we never imagined we would," Declan commented, his deep voice soft, kind even. "Wilson bonded with Rory's younger brother, Brennan, so he and Kendra are part of my pack, too."

"Really?" Sheridan snapped open his eyes and glanced from Rory to Declan and back again. When Rory nodded, he couldn't help but ask, "Is that why Wilson filed for a divorce?" Disgust caused his gut to twist. "Was he cheating on my sister?"

While Sheridan didn't agree with Shandell's decision to burn their house down, regardless of her reasoning, he still felt indignation on her behalf. He knew his sister was cut from a similar cloth as Spencer. Still, she *was* his sister.

"No," Rory denied. "Wilson was already looking into divorce lawyers before meeting Brennan." He grimaced as he added, "I know she's yer sister, Sher, but she's not a nice woman or a good mother."

Sheridan winced upon hearing Rory's opinion of his sister. Biting his lip, he huffed a breath through his nose. He didn't want to fight with the man, especially knowing he was right.

"In our pack, we have something called restitution," Dixon stated, drawing Sheridan's attention. His blue eyes held a serious gleam, and his full lips were pressed in a thin line. "Do you know the term?"

Slowly, Sheridan shook his head. "What's that?" He didn't want to seem ignorant, but he would need to hear the word in a sentence to hazard a guess.

"It means Wilson can ask for compensation for the damage you did to him . . . physical and emotional," Dixon explained, leaning forward and resting his forearms on his thick thighs. "Right now, all he wants is for you to leave him and Kendra alone while they move on with their lives."

Sheridan swallowed hard as pain stabbed through his chest. He nodded, understanding. His last free family wanted nothing to do with him.

It's what I deserve.

"I'll leave them alone," Sheridan promised. Meeting Dixon's gaze, he murmured, "Will you at least tell him I'm sorry?"

"I will," Dixon agreed.

"There's more," Declan stated. "Because Rory and Brennan are brothers, it could make it awkward at pack and family functions, because ye'll both be there." He narrowed his eyes as he tipped his head. "I've asked Wilson to be respectful, and I ask the same of you." Then the corners of his lips twitched. "And if they initiate contact with ye, ye're welcome to respond. I have a feeling Kendra will miss ye before too long. She enjoys the way ye play dolls with her."

Sheridan smiled, recalling those times. "It was fun."

"And ye're to go to counseling." Declan smiled at him. "We get that ye're as much a victim in this as Wilson and Kendra. Living under Spencer's thumb couldn't have been easy."

Gaping, Sheridan couldn't believe the understanding expressions on the faces of those around him. He had never experienced such . . . acceptance. The backs of his eyes began to burn, and he blinked quickly as he swallowed hard.

These shifters are offering me more than my own family ever did. Just . . . damn!

Still—

After clearing his throat, Sheridan met the alpha's gaze. "I'm pretty sure I know where each of the pieces upstairs came from. Spencer would have me catalog them and estimate their values." Some of the jewelry had been damn expensive. Hunching, he added, "I, uh, I just don't know how to return it to people without turning myself in."

"Don't worry," Manon assured him. "We'll take care of a cover story." He chuckled. "We're good at those."

Sheridan didn't know what to think of that, so he just nodded.

"Let's head upstairs, then." Declan set Lark on his feet, then stood next to him. "We'll get started on going through Spencer's stolen jewelry." He turned and ordered, "Manon, give Raul a call and let him know all we've learned. I want a trace on Payne's number. He may be using a burner, but if not, I want a location." As Declan headed toward the stairs, he added, "And Dixon, give Clancy a call and see how the case against Shandell is coming. I heard she didn't post bail due to the crime involved, and we don't want anything to jeopardize that."

Sheridan didn't know who those other people were, but he figured he would learn at some point.

Or I can ask Rory about it, eventually.

Dismissing the thought, Sheridan heaved to his feet. When Rory did the same and immediately took his hand, a tingle went up his arm. He couldn't help but smile up at the bigger man.

"Come on, my mate," Rory urged. "Let's show the jewelry to the alpha. Then we can pack up anything ye want." Grinning, he added, "Especially yer carvings. They're exquisite. Where did ye learn to do that?"

Sheridan followed Alpha Declan and Gracen upstairs. He felt his heart flutter in his chest at the praise. His neck warmed, and he knew he was blushing again.

Except, this time, it was a good feeling.

"I taught myself," Sheridan admitted.

"Damn." Rory squeezed his hand. "I can't wait to hear all about that."

Sheridan squeezed back, liking the contact oh-so-much.

CHAPTER SIX

Rory forced down the disgust he felt for Spencer. There wasn't a point to the feeling. The man was dead.

Too bad. I would very happily kill him for the life he forced on my mate.

Spencer had made a pigsty out of the home's huge master suite. Fortunately, he hadn't demanded Sheridan clean it as he had the rest of the house. Well, to be fair, Spencer hadn't *demanded* Sheridan clean. He just didn't clean anything on his own, and Sheridan had picked up the slack.

My mate is a good man, regardless of what he's been forced to do in the past.

Reaching over the space between them in his *Bronco*, Rory took Sheridan's hand. He squeezed lightly before bringing their twined fingers to his lips. After nibbling one of Sheridan's knuckles lightly, he placed them on the bench seat between them.

"I'm certain ye have questions." Rory glanced Sheridan's way before returning his focus to the road. It was starting to snow again, and he didn't want to get into an accident. "Anything ye want to know?"

"How is your alpha going to get all that stuff back to the owners?" Sheridan rubbed his free hand on the thigh of his jeans, picking at the worn fabric. "I know I deserve to go to jail, but" — he heaved a sigh before mumbling — "I really don't want to."

"I'm not letting ye end up in jail," Rory vowed. "And neither will my pack. We'll fake yer death and give ye a new

46

identity before it comes to that."

Leaning toward him, Sheridan gaped for a few seconds. "Really? You can do that?"

"We can." Knowing he needed to share more, he added, "And we do often."

"Why?"

Rory flashed a grin Sheridan's way as he explained, "We said paranormals live for a long time. I'm a little over a hundred. Barring injury, I should live until I'm about five hundred . . . give or take a couple of decades."

"Holy shit!"

Hearing the squeak in Sheridan's voice, Rory chuckled. "Every few decades, we end the life of our identity and create a new one. Most of the time, that involves us dropping off the grid for a decade so any humans that know us well will forget about us." Releasing Sheridan's hand, he turned on his blinker, so he could take the turn-off to Stone Ridge. "I hear vampires will often change covens every few decades, but shifters aren't like that. Unless we have an issue with our pack, we'll most likely stay in the same one all our lives."

"Centuries," Sheridan whispered. "Wow." An uneasy note entered his voice as he asked, "How do you know you'll want to be with me all that time? Or do shifters dissolve a mate-bond if it doesn't work out?"

Rory growled low in his throat, possessiveness shooting through him at the idea of *dissolving a mate-bond*. It didn't matter that it couldn't be done. The fact that Sheridan even asked about it pissed him off.

Tightening his grip a little, Rory rumbled, "No. A shifter cannot dissolve a bond between fated mates." He glanced Sheridan's way and added, "Like us."

"But—"

"No buts, Sheridan." Still scenting his mate's concern and confusion, Rory hurried to add, "A shifter is hard-wired to please and care for his fated mate, no matter what." Smirking at him, he added, "For example, if ye really had been someone who had aggressive tendencies, I would have found ways to help ye control them as well as giving ye alternate outlets for them."

"Alternate outlets?" Sheridan scoffed. "How is there an alternate outlet for the desire to beat the shit out of someone just because you can?"

Rory opened his mouth, then closed it again. After a moment of thought, he decided on, "First, counseling, so we could discover the reason behind yer desire." With a wink, he continued, "Then I'd learn yoga and meditation with ye. We could enjoy boxing or tai chi. From what I hear, many martial arts are about control just as much as power, and they teach ye how to use as little force as possible to take out yer opponent."

"Huh." Sheridan bobbed his head a little, processing that. "Okay. So, um, we're it for each other, then? Because Fate decided?" When Rory glanced at his mate again, Sheridan's brows were furrowed. "It's such an odd thing to believe."

"Not really," Rory countered. "Fate lets a shifter know who their best match is, but we would have been attracted regardless." He hissed as his *Bronco* slid a little on a patch of ice. Blowing out a breath, he muttered, "Colorado mountain winters. Gotta love 'em."

"Yeah." Sheridan had moved his grip to the *oh shit* handled. "How far past Stone Ridge is this cabin?"

"Only about fifteen miles, but it's winding roads, so it takes a little while," Rory revealed. Then, recalling something else he hadn't shared, he absently added, "Besides, paranormals are pretty sexual by nature, and once we bond with our fated mate, we can't even get it up for another." Risking another glance at his mate, Rory swept his gaze over Sheridan's lean form. "I'll enjoy exploring ye over and over again, handsome mate."

Sheridan once again gaped at him. "You can't even get it up?"

Rory shook his head.

"What if your fated mate rejects you?"

Just the suggestion caused Rory's gut to clench. "We would have to wait until that fated mate died of old age before getting the chance at meeting another." Swallowing hard, he whispered, "Please don't reject me, Sheridan." His hands tightened on the wheel as his heart began to thunder in his chest. "I know this is confusing to ye, but—"

"Hey, hey. I'm sorry I said that," Sheridan cried, placing a hand on his arm. "I didn't say I was going to reject you. It was just a random, stupid question." Massaging Rory's tight bicep, Sheridan grumbled under his breath, "Shit. What a dumb thing to say."

Placing his hand over Sheridan's, Rory squeezed as his arms relaxed. He blew out a breath and shook his head. "No, I'm sorry. I, uh, I overreacted. I shouldn't have jumped to conclusions." He squeezed Sheridan's fingers again before returning his hand to the wheel. "You have every right to ask any question that ye wish."

Sheridan nodded, but he didn't say anything more for several minutes.

They arrived in Stone Ridge, and Rory turned his *Bronco* into the parking lot of the town market. "We'll buy enough groceries for a few days. Unfortunately, if the plan is to work, ye need to be seen around here."

Even as Sheridan followed him into the store, he murmured, "How is he going to know that I'm heading this way, again?"

Winking, Rory took his hand and threaded their fingers together as the automatic door opened. "Ye left a copy of our dinner reservation for two on yer bed." He pointed toward the street behind them. "It's for Caribou's, located in Stone Ridge. We'll be going to dinner there tomorrow evening."

"Oh." Rory scented Sheridan's nerves and felt his mate tug on his hand. "Relax," he urged, squeezing his fingers. "People here are damn accepting." Dipping his head, he whispered, "At least half of the people who work here are pack or related to pack, and half the pack are gay."

Sheridan stared up at him with wide eyes. "Geez. Really?"

"Mmm-hmmm," Rory confirmed before turning his attention to the aisles. "So, got any favorite foods I should know about?" Then he snapped his fingers. "And don't forget to call Randy so he knows ye're quitting."

Rory was beyond pleased by that fact. His mate was moving to Stone Ridge. It worked out well, since Wilson was staying in Colin City for the next few years. It would give the pair time to heal their relationship . . . as much as possible, anyway.

Having met Wilson and Kendra on numerous occasions, Rory bet that it wouldn't be long before they hashed it all out.

"Oh, right," Sheridan muttered, pulling out his phone.

"After shopping," Rory stated, gripping his wrist. He feared how nasty Randy could be and didn't want his mate upset in public. "Let's check out the ice cream. Are ye allergic to anything?"

As Rory pushed the small cart down the aisle before him, he paused to grab marshmallows, chocolate bars, and graham crackers. Then he began toward the freezer section. Sheridan still hadn't answered when he reached the pizza section.

Pausing, Rory focused on his mate. "Sheridan?"

Sheridan rubbed the back of his neck, frowning. "I've always bought the brands Spencer liked, so I'm really not sure."

"Oh, yeah?" *Bastard.* "What brand pizza was that?"

Pointing, Sheridan indicated a sausage lover's style pie. "Okay."

Rory avoided that one and stepped to the next door. He opened it and grabbed a pepperoni pizza, then a chicken alfredo option. After putting them in the cart, he opened another door and pulled out microwavable pepperoni pockets plus a couple of boxes of single-serving pepperoni pizzas on French bread slices. Upon seeing Sheridan's surprised expression, Rory winked.

"So, what about macaroni and cheese?" Rory asked, starting them down the aisle again. "I love it with hot dogs. Simple and tasty. Or would ye prefer sausage alfredo?" Spotting something else he loved, he reached into another freezer case. "Curly fries to bake as well as hot wings."

As Rory placed both into their cart, Sheridan barked a soft laugh. "I thought we were just getting stuff for a few days."

Leaning close, Rory whispered, "Shifters eat a lot." Then he waggled his brows. "Plus, I intend to help ye work up an appetite."

Upon seeing the slight flush staining Sheridan's cheeks, Rory grinned.

Yep. My man caught my meaning.

Rory could hardly wait until he had the chance to explore his mate's sweet body . . . for hours. As they moved through a few more aisles, he tossed different stuff into the cart—frozen cinnamon rolls, beer, wine, and more.

"So . . . ye still haven't told me if ye have any favorites." Rory rubbed his hand down his spine and asked, "On the rare occasion ye may not have been providing for Spencer, what was your *go to*?"

"Chocolate chip cookie dough ice cream," Sheridan finally told him.

Grinning widely, Rory hummed. "Nice choice." He found the desired ice cream and put a large carton into the cart. Then he crossed to the fresh meat section. "Got a favorite cut?"

Sheridan scoffed. "No."

Rory figured that was a silly question. *Oh well.* "Then let's get a few."

Even as Sheridan protested, Rory ignored it and picked out a couple of New York strip steaks, top sirloin, and T-bones. Then he led the way out of the freezer and cooler area. When they reached the cereal aisle, Rory grabbed a box of *Cocoa Puffs*.

"Anything ye want?" Rory pointed vaguely at the myriad of choices.

After a few seconds of hesitation, Sheridan grabbed a box of *Golden Grahams*.

Rory groaned. "Nice. My second favorite." He winked. "Ye gonna share?"

Sheridan's brows shot up as he met Rory's gaze. "Y-Yes?"

Chuckling, Rory commented. "Ye don't sound sure." He grabbed a second box of the serial. With a wink, he stated, "Just in case."

Staring at the box, Sheridan licked his lips. The scent of anticipation perfumed the air.

Gods, I love providing for my mate.

"What kind of milk do ye prefer?"

Sheridan shoved his hands into his pockets. "I prefer skim, but Spencer wanted two-percent."

Rory nodded. He grabbed a carton of skim as well as one vitamin D. Finally, they ended up at the fresh fruit and veggies section.

To Rory's pleasure, Sheridan reached out and took something without prompting.

Smiling, Rory watched him fill a bag with several plums. He filled a bag of his own with a few peaches. After snagging some green grapes and half a dozen ears of corn, he pointed at the cauliflower and strawberries.

"Interested?"

"I like both," Sheridan confirmed, but his gaze had strayed to something else.

Brussel sprouts. Huh.

"Ye want them instead?" They weren't one of Rory's favorites, but he didn't mind them. He grabbed another bag and prepared to pick up a handful.

"Yeah." Sheridan smiled. "I haven't had any since before my mom died. Spencer hated them."

"Then we'll get enough for a couple of meals."

Once Rory had paid for their purchases, he led the way outside. The snow had picked up, falling steadily. He reached in and started his *Bronco* before opening the back door.

When Sheridan moved to help him load the groceries inside, Rory offered, "Why don't ye hop in and make yer phone call? I doubt ye'll get service at the cabin. I don't."

Even as Sheridan nodded and climbed in the passenger side, he asked, "If you don't get service, how will we call for help when Payne shows up?"

Rory just stopped himself from snorting. The day he would need help taking out one human was the day he didn't deserve a mate. He didn't say that, however.

Instead, Rory grinned at Sheridan and told him, "I have a satellite phone."

"Oh." Then Sheridan lifted his phone to his ear.

A few seconds later, Rory heard Randy answer. "It's about time you called me back. Didn't your friend give you the message?"

"I'm sorry, Randy," Sheridan replied, his voice subdued. "It's been a rough couple of days. I —"

"I don't care about that," Randy cut in. "If you can't keep your problems from impacting my business, don't bother coming in the morning."

Rory clenched his jaw as he placed the last bag of groceries into his *Bronco*. Just before he closed the back door, he heard Sheridan state, "Yes, sir. I won't."

As Rory climbed behind the wheel, he heard Randy demand, "You won't what? Let your problems impact my business?"

"No, sir," Sheridan countered. He reached over and, to Rory's pleasure, initiated touch for the first time, threading their fingers together. "I won't bother coming in the morning."

"What?" Randy barked. "After the break I gave you? You selfish prick. Don't ask for a reference. You—"

Sheridan lowered the phone, disconnecting the call in the process. While his heavy sigh wasn't surprising, his lips curving into a slight smile was. Then he grinned at Rory.

Chuckling, Rory asked, "How'd that feel?"

"Damn good. Thank you." Sheridan shook his head. "He was always such a prick. I can't figure out how he keeps any servers."

Rory barked a laugh as he shook his head. "Good question." He squeezed Sheridan's leg, then pulled on his seatbelt. "Let's get to the cabin before this storm gets worse."

Even as Sheridan nodded, he asked worriedly, "Are you sure it's safe?"

Nodding, Rory assured, "We'll make it."

He refused to think otherwise because he needed to get his mate alone as soon as possible.

CHAPTER SEVEN

Sheridan didn't think the tension left his shoulders until the shape of a cabin came into view, barely discernable through the darkness and falling snow. When Rory stopped the vehicle before the shady outline, Sheridan heaved a deep sigh.

"Holy shit," he mumbled, peeling his fingers from the *oh shit* handle. "We made it."

Rory chuckled. "It wasn't that bad."

Groaning, Sheridan frowned at the other man. "Yes, it was."

Continuing to snicker, Rory winked at him. "I won't take that as an insult to my driving."

"No, it was an insult to your city's road maintenance," Sheridan grumbled.

Barking another laugh, Rory grinned at him. "Ready to brave the cold?"

"Do I have a choice?"

Rory teased the tips of his forefingers along Sheridan's jaw. "No, my mate, but I'm enjoying yer snark." Then he leaned forward and pecked a kiss to his lips. "Stay here just a sec while I get the door open. Then we'll each take in an armload of groceries."

Sheridan couldn't find his tongue, similar to every time Rory kissed him. Instead, he just nodded. After another quick kiss, Rory slipped from the *Bronco*.

For the couple of seconds that the door was open, a deep gust of air swirled through the cab.

Hunching his shoulders, Sheridan grimaced. His coat was in no way thick enough for the current weather. He wondered if Rory would expect him to do much outside.

Hope not.

Sheridan leaned forward and squinted through the windshield. Rory had left the lights on, so he was able to watch the bigger man's outline. The guy trudged through the two-foot deep snow and onto the porch. After unlocking the door, he entered. He was gone for what felt like forever before a warm glow flowed out the door. Rory reappeared, leaving the door open just a smidge, and headed back to his vehicle.

Before Rory reached it, Sheridan took a deep breath and shoved open his door. He shivered even before exiting. Still, he knew it was necessary, so he hopped from the vehicle. Then Sheridan slammed the door shut and hustled around to the back.

Shifting from foot to foot, he watched Rory open the door. Then he quickly grabbed as many bags as he could before hopping in the other man's boot prints. He remembered his manners just before crossing the threshold.

Sheridan paused and tapped his sneaker-clad feet against the door frame, doing his best to knock off as much snow as he could.

"Damn, I forgot ye were in sneakers," Rory muttered from directly behind him. "In ye get." Then he pressed his front to Sheridan's back, pressing him forward.

Feeling Rory's package nudging him, Sheridan gasped and jolted forward.

Holy shit! He's not soft. He was just walking through an almost blizzard. How is that even possible?

Sheridan had no idea, but it was a fact. A glance back and down confirmed it. The thud of the grocery bags hitting the wood floor snapped Sheridan's gaze upward.

Rory stared at him with narrowed eyes and a hungry expression. "I really, *really* like the way ye're looking at me,

Sher."

The heat in his tone caused a wash of heat to flood Sheridan's veins. He opened his mouth, but then a gust of air swirled into the cabin.

Grimacing, Rory leaned down and pecked a kiss to Sheridan's lips. "Hold onto that thought," he murmured. "If ye don't mind, will ye take these to the kitchen and put them away?" He pointed at the groceries he'd left on the floor. "There's a couple more bags along with the beer and wine we chose. I'll grab them before heading around back."

Even as Sheridan nodded, he asked, "What's around back?"

"Access to the cupboard that houses the hot water heater and propane. I'll fire those up, then bring in firewood." Rory pointed at a large wood-burning fireplace. "This is a small cabin and heated with that. I'll start a fire next."

"Wow. Okay." Sheridan couldn't remember a time he hadn't had actual heat. "That'd be great."

Rory nodded. "Be back in a jiffy."

After Rory strode back into the dark, Sheridan turned and peered around the place again. He spotted the oil lantern sitting on the kitchen counter and headed that way. That took him through a small living space with a couple of old sofas and with a bearskin rug before the fireplace. He also noticed a rack with a number of books, games, and puzzles stacked on it. Due to the dim lightly, he couldn't make out any of the titles, though.

Something to explore later.

Sheridan loved things that engaged his mind. He wished he could have taken computer courses, but his brother had scoffed when he'd expressed his desire. Then Spencer had smacked him upside the head — hard — and told him, "This family ain't got no use for a geek."

I wonder what Rory would say if I shared my interest.

Not quite ready to find out, Sheridan pushed the memory

aside. He focused on doing what Rory had asked of him. After placing the bags he carried on the kitchen counter, he began opening all the cupboard doors, so he could learn where everything went.

Once Sheridan had found a spot for everything, he returned to the door and grabbed another armload. He spotted the beer, wine, and another couple of bags next to the now-closed door. He realized he'd been so long in his head that he hadn't even heard Rory return.

Sheridan stacked all the items in the freezer and fridge. When he heard the clunk of something followed by a hum, he cocked his head. After another second, he heard the trudge of footsteps on snow before a knock sounded on the back door, which was located through a small mud-room.

After lifting a hook from a metal eye, Sheridan unlocked it and pulled the door open. He found a shivering, snow-covered Rory, his arms full of logs, on the other side. The wind swooping in through the door caused an answering shudder in Sheridan's body, so he quickly backed a step and moved out of his way.

"Damn, it looks cold out there," Sheridan commented as he closed the door behind him. "Think we'll get snowed in?"

"Hope not, since we're supposed to go on that date tomorrow," Rory replied as he trudged across the cabin, snow falling from his boots. After placing the wood to the left of a grate that already held a half-dozen dry logs, he turned his head and winked at Sheridan. "But it wouldn't be the worst thing in the world. Don't worry. I'd keep ye warm." Then Rory gave him a lascivious once-over that told him exactly how the bigger man intended to keep him warm.

Unable to help himself, Sheridan chuckled even as a blush heated his cheeks. He gathered his courage and offered, "Um, well . . . maybe you can teach me how to reciprocate?"

Rory froze where he was laying wood, kindling, and paper

to start the fire. Peering at him with wide eyes, he whispered, "Y-Ye've never—"

Sheridan didn't need Rory to finish his question. He shrugged, then shook his head. He figured he ought to be honest about his lack of experience.

Groaning, Rory reached down and adjusted himself. He swallowed so hard his Adam's apple bobbed. "Oh, Sher. Oh, my mate." His husky voice betrayed how much he liked that fact even more than his narrowed eyes and flaring nostrils. "I can't wait to teach ye everything, show ye everything, share everything with ye."

A tremble of answering need trickled down Sheridan's spine. Heat coursed through his veins, warming him better than any fire. He barely resisted the urge to adjust himself as his dick thickened behind his fly.

Moaning, Rory shook his head. "Gods, my mate," he muttered as he returned his focus to the fire. "Warm the house first. Don't want ye to freeze when I make love to ye."

Make love? Does that mean he loves me?

Sheridan shook his head. "No," he mumbled to himself. "That's just an expression."

"Did ye say something, handsome?"

Shaking his head, Sheridan replied, "No. No." Then he finished putting the groceries away.

Sheridan hadn't even heard Rory move, so when he felt the man's arms slide around his waist from behind, he jerked forward.

"Easy, Sher," Rory purred into his ear while he tightened his hold. "Ye're okay. It's just me."

Relaxing slowly, Sheridan turned his head just a little. He could just make out Rory's features in the dim lighting. "Not used to touch," Sheridan admitted. "I—" He paused, uncertain how much more he should say, so he just shrugged.

"I hope it's something ye'll be okay working on, Sheridan," Rory murmured, sliding his fingers under the bottom of his

59

jacket and teasing over his cloth-covered belly. "Because I really like touching you."

Shivers worked across Sheridan's skin, and his tummy trembled. His skin goose bumped, and a groan slipped passed his lips. The hairs on his arms stood on end as tingles washed over his body.

Gripping Rory's forearms, Sheridan opened and closed his mouth. He had no idea what to say or do. Never in his life had he experienced such sensations.

Finally, Sheridan managed to process Rory's comments, and he swallowed, forcing moisture to his dry throat. "Yes," he muttered. "Yes, I like your touch."

"Good." Rory nuzzled his lips along Sheridan's neck.

Sheridan didn't know if he trembled due to their coldness or from the fiery tendrils of need thrumming through him.

Rory licked a line up Sheridan's neck before starting, "Do you—"

The rumble of Sheridan's belly interrupted him.

Chuckling, Rory finished, "—hungry?"

While Sheridan doubted that was what Rory had actually been ready to say, he still answered, "Yes." It was obvious anyway. Besides, he figured it had to have been over twenty-four hours since he'd eaten anything substantial.

"I'll start up the oven. It takes a little while to warm, especially the first time out of the gate," Rory warned, drawing away from him. "So how about we eat dessert first in front of the fire?"

Sheridan couldn't stop his grin. "Dessert first?"

Rory waggled his eyebrows. "Yep. That tasty ice cream ye chose."

When Sheridan's stomach grumbled again, Rory laughed. He slid around him in the small kitchen and turned on the propane knob. After muttering to the count of three, he gripped a different knob and turned it.

A loud click sounded through the cabin.

Crouching down, Rory appeared to be searching for something near the base of the oven. He must not have seen it, for he reached up and turned the second knob again. That time, a soft rushing, roaring sound came from the oven. Then lines of pale blue flame could barely be seen inside the space.

"Sweet." Rory stood and adjusted the first knob to the highest setting. Immediately, the blue flames flared up along rows at the bottom of the oven. As Rory closed the oven door, he straightened. "Okay. We'll give that ten minutes."

"What do you do if that starter knob doesn't work?" Sheridan asked curiously. He'd never seen a propane oven before.

Rory pointed at the fireplace. "Get a stick and light it manually."

Sheridan gaped. "Isn't that dangerous."

"Naw." Rory shook his head. "That's why ye keep the propane low at first."

"Oh."

Rory crossed to the fire and added another couple of logs. Then he took off his coat and hung it on a hook near the front door. Next, he kicked off his boots and placed them on a plastic mat nearby.

Finally, Rory picked up a towel and began mopping up the melting snow on the floor.

"I can do that," Sheridan claimed, feeling uncomfortable just standing around.

Flashing a smile his way, Rory shook his head. "Go stand by the fire and warm up. Ye're jacket and sneakers aren't warm enough for this weather."

Sheridan did as he'd been told. As he stood before the fire, the heat sinking into his bones, the occasional shiver that he hadn't even noticed finally stopped. He sighed deeply and closed his eyes.

Fatigue rolled through him, and he began to sway.

Snapping his eyelids open, Sheridan shook his head. His stomach grumbled again. No way did he want to fall asleep before food. That would mean he would feel like shit the next day.

"Have ye decided what ye want to eat?" Rory asked where he still knelt on the floor. "Got lots of pizza, wings, fries. I'd advise holding off on the lasagna. It'll take forever to cook." Grinning up at him, Rory offered, "We'll have to plan ahead for that one. Maybe the day after tomorrow."

"Pizza and fries," Sheridan blurted out. "Can we do that?"

"Sounds dee-lish," Rory replied, drawing out the second word before licking his lips. "Which pizza ye want?"

"A-Any of them?" Sheridan asked, suddenly feeling wary. *Is this a test?*

Rory paused for an instant, his head snapping up as he re-focused on him. "Yes, my mate," he replied softly. "I like everything I put in the cart."

Sheridan suddenly feared he'd hurt the man's feelings, considering the tight lines that appeared at the corners of his lips. "Um, I've never had pizza with chicken and white sauce."

When a wide grin stretched his lips, Rory winked. "You got it. Okay, let's toss those pepperoni French bread singles in there, too. Ye can try a couple of flavors." Humming, he swiped the towel over the floor one last time before standing. "And I know we have brand new bottles of mayo and ketchup on the shelf in the back. I'll make fry sauce for the curly fries." Rory groaned as he disappeared in the mud-room, but Sheridan still heard his mutterings. "Damn, now I'm starving, too."

Rory returned without the towel, but he held a bottle in each hand. When he set them on the counter, Sheridan saw that they were the aforementioned items. Excitement coursed through Sheridan at the prospect of trying all those different foods.

Deciding he was warm enough, he unzipped his jacket and

hung it on a coat hook. Not wanting to track water over Rory's freshly cleaned floor, he toed off his sneakers, too. He grabbed his bag, which Rory had also set by the door at some point, and carried it to the sofa.

Sheridan quickly dug out another pair of socks. Then he sat down and pulled off his damp ones, replacing them with the clean, dry pair. After that, he stuck his feet toward the fire and sighed.

"Want me to take those?" Rory offered, moving toward him. "There's a washer and dryer in the back. I can't run it now, because it's powered by a gas generator we have in case of emergencies, but I'll get 'em clean for ye eventually."

Sheridan handed off his socks. "Thanks."

"Yep." Then Rory trailed his fingertips over Sheridan's nape as he said, "Wanna come help me decide how many fries to bake?"

Happy with the offer to do something, Sheridan nodded and rose to his feet.

Chapter Eight

Rory took in the release of tension in Sheridan's shoulders, and he knew he'd made the right choice.

It seems my mate has a tough time sitting around while another does something.

He figured that had everything to do with living with Spencer.

Pulling out the chicken pizza box, Rory handed it to Sheridan. "There's scissors in the drawer to the right of the sink. Or feel free to use a knife from the block over there."

Rory pointed. Then he headed into the mud-room to retrieve a cookie sheet. The right wall of the space was covered in shelves and cubbies filled with all sorts of items from cooking to baking to cleaning. Everything that wasn't re-sealable was stored in a zipper bag or canister.

After choosing a cookie sheet and a canister of olive oil baking spray, Rory returned to the kitchen. He held the sheet over the sink, then sprayed it. Leaving it on the counter, he returned the spray to its place on the shelf.

Seeing that Sheridan had finished opening the pizza, Rory pulled both the fries and the French bread pizzas out of the freezer. He handed the box that contained the two pizzas to Sheridan, then took the scissors he'd left on the counter. With a few quick snips, Rory had the bag open, so he handed the shears back to a waiting Sheridan.

Rory held up the bag. "Do ye want me to measure out a few servings?" He winked. "Or should I just cook them all?"

Sheridan moaned softly as he licked his lips. His stomach

64

growled once more. Still, he shook his head as he looked at the food on the counter, ready to go into the oven.

"You really think we'll be able to eat it all?"

Chuckling, Rory nodded. "Oh yeah." After knocking his shoulder lightly against his mate's, he reminded, "Shifters have huge appetites."

"Oh, right." Sheridan nodded, then shrugged. "Okay. All of it sounds great."

Rory was more than on board with that. He knew that, even though the bag said it contained eight servings, he could easily consume two-thirds of it on his own. Coupled with the two types of pizza, he figured their meal would be just about the right size—seeing as he wasn't starving or anything.

"So, how long did the different boxes say for cooking time?" Rory asked as he dumped the entire contents of the bag onto the tray. They almost fell over the sides, but he quickly caught them. Looking at the back, Rory told Sheridan, "This says twelve to fifteen minutes."

"The chicken pizza is supposed to be cooked for twenty," Sheridan told him. Then he frowned as he looked at the other box. "These other ones need eighteen."

"Okay." Rory grabbed the cardboard the chicken pizza rested on and turned around. He opened the oven and peered at the racks. "Hmm. Hold this."

Sheridan obeyed, taking the pizza.

Rory quickly snagged a couple of oven mitts from a nearby drawer, pulling them on. Then he adjusted the three racks. After removing the gloves, he placed the chicken pizza on the lowest shelf. The fries went on the top, and the pizza singles ended up in the middle.

While it wasn't an exact science, and Rory intended to check them every five minutes after the first ten, he'd seen his mother use the technique enough times to know it worked.

Once Rory had everything in, he winked at Sheridan and

pointed toward the mud-room. "Garbage is in there. Will ye break down the boxes and toss everything, please?"

Sheridan quickly got to work with a smile and a nod.

Rory's gut clenched at seeing the immediate obedience. He wasn't a dominant wolf by any means, but as the shifter in the relationship, his wolf felt a definite desire to be the one in charge. Having seen other pairings in the pack where the human was more dominant, Rory wasn't certain how his own would go, but he loved the feeling that he was caring for his human.

Returning to the freezer one more time, Rory pulled out the tub of ice cream. He plopped it on the counter and grabbed two spoons from the drawer. When Sheridan returned to the room, he waggled his brows as he held one out.

"Ready for the first course?"

Sheridan glanced between the spoons and the ice cream and grinned broadly. Taking it, he hummed enthusiastically. Then he glanced over the counter.

"Bowls?"

Rory shook his head. "No bowls. Come on."

Grabbing the tub, Rory led the way into the living room. He sat down on the bearskin rug and placed the ice cream on the floor before him. Then he quickly set a timer on his phone.

By then, Sheridan had joined him on the floor. "Are we really going to eat it right out of the container?"

Hearing how scandalized Sheridan sounded by the idea, Rory laughed. "Oh, yeah. As much or as little as ye want," he told him with a wink.

Sheridan opened his mouth, then closed it again.

Rory opened the ice cream tub and set aside the lid. Then he slid his spoon through the creamy goodness. He held out the tub as he slid the spoon into his mouth.

The tasty cold treat hit his taste buds, making him hum with pleasure. The chocolate chip gave the bite a pleasant crunch, while the bit of cookie dough contrasted deliciously. He licked his spoon clean as he watched Sheridan carefully make up his own spoonful.

"So, ye taught yerself whittling," Rory commented as he helped himself to another spoonful of ice cream. "Did ye read books?" He didn't remember seeing any on whittling in Sheridan's room, but he hadn't stuck around too long to read all the titles. "Or watched videos online?"

Sheridan had just been shoving his own bite of ice cream into his mouth, so Rory waited patiently. Seeing his mate's expression of absolute pleasure coupled with his moan of appreciation caused his blood to rush south. Rory nearly swayed where he sat as his big head emptied.

Day-um!

Rory shoved his own spoon into his mouth to keep himself from saying something stupid . . . or something his mate might not be ready to hear.

After Sheridan swallowed, he answered. "My mom bought me my first *how to* book, although my dad hoped it would morph into me loving carpentry." Shaking his head, he scooped up more ice cream. "It didn't. They died in a car crash on a slippery, snow-covered road the winter after I graduated." Sheridan stared at his full spoon as he murmured, "Mom died immediately in the crash, but Dad lived just long enough in the hospital to remind us that it was our responsibility to care for Shandell. Spencer really took that to heart, even after she married."

"Damn, baby," Rory murmured, reaching over and gripping his wrist. He squeezed lightly. "I'm so sorry."

Sheridan shrugged again. Then a forced-looking smile curved his lips. "I carve to remember Mom." Frowning, he muttered, "And Spencer twisted my love for it into something . . . horrible."

Rory knew Sheridan was thinking about how he'd been forced to alter stolen jewelry. Uncertain what to say, he just squeezed his human's wrist again. Fortunately, the chime of his phone saved him.

"Gonna see how our food is doing."

Stabbing his spoon in the ice cream again, Rory scooped some up before rising to his feet. As he headed into the kitchen, he shoved the bite into his mouth. The tasty treat didn't taste quite so wonderful anymore.

Fucking Spencer.

Rory knew it would take years—hell, maybe even decades—before certain memories wouldn't be tainted by the man. He hoped the counseling Declan had ordered would help. Rory intended to join his mate, once he was ready.

With the intent of building happy memories together, Rory called, "So just books? Some of those pieces were absolutely exquisite. Do ye sell any of them?" As he pulled on the oven mitts, Rory told his mate, "There's a few small stores in town that would probably allow ye to set up a display. And a couple of the restaurants are owned by pack-mates. They'd let ye set up a display there, too."

As Rory opened the oven door and checked on the different items, he heard Sheridan rise. A couple of thumps sounded in the cabin, followed by a shower of crackles. Straightening and turning, Rory smiled, seeing his mate had been feeding the fire.

When Sheridan turned to face him, his expression appeared thoughtful. "I've sold a few online," he admitted. "I have a website. The money goes into a *PayPal* account I opened a few years ago." Shoving his hands into his pockets, Sheridan admitted, "Once the account hit five K, I was gonna try running again. My pieces don't sell for much, so it was taking a long time. This fiasco with Wilson just sped up my timetable."

Rory felt his heart trip in his chest. He could only imagine how difficult sharing that information had been for Sheridan. It was beyond apparent that his mate was a damn private, skittish person.

But he trusts me.

Grinning, Rory crooned, "That is damn impressive, Sheridan." Leaning on the counter, he couldn't help but ask, "If ye don't mind me asking, what do ye charge for them?"

"I don't mind," Sheridan answered, heading toward the kitchen. He held the ice cream in one hand and his spoon in the other. "Here. Don't want to eat too much, or I won't have room for pizza."

Understanding, Rory took it and put it away.

Once Rory had straightened, Sheridan leaned a hip against the counter and told him, "Between four-ninety-nine and eight-ninety-nine plus shipping and handling. Normally people will buy two or three at a time." Shrugging, he told him, "I started it just over two years ago when I began running out of room for my sculptures."

With how many Rory had still seen in the room, he couldn't imagine how many more there must have been. He didn't say as such, though. Instead, he offered, "I'll talk to a couple of people around town. I know a few places sell local art. This wouldn't be any different."

Sheridan's smile was small but appeared genuine. "Thank you."

"Ye're welcome." As Rory spoke, he reached out and threaded his fingers through Sheridan's short hair. He dipped his head, taking in the way his mate's lips parted and how his breathing sped up.

Then his phone chimed, indicating it'd been another five minutes.

Chuckling softly, Rory still pressed a peck to his lips. "That food is really starting to smell good." The scent of pizza and the seasonings on the fries perfumed the air.

"Yeah," Sheridan whispered, agreeing with him.

Rory grabbed the hot pads again and once more checked the food. "It looks like everything needs just a few more minutes." Grinning, he closed the door and took off the pads. "Let's make the fry sauce."

Stepping closer to Sheridan, Rory rested his left hand on his mate's hip. As he massaged under his shirt just a little, he leaned closer. He raised his right arm and opened the cupboard door near Sheridan's head.

By feel, Rory grabbed a soup bowl and pulled it out. Before setting it down, he pressed his lips against Sheridan's. Even though Rory knew he didn't have much time, he couldn't resist dipping in his tongue and getting a taste of the man he soon planned to make his lover — for all time.

Too bad I can't linger . . . but I will later.

Rory eased the much too short kiss to an end, then rubbed his nose along Sheridan's in an eskimo kiss. "Soon I'm gonna take my time tasting ye're entire body."

As Rory felt Sheridan tremble under his hold, he groaned before releasing him. "Ye're too delicious, my mate." Then he set about whipping together the fry sauce.

Once that was done, Rory offered it to Sheridan. "Wanna dip ye're finger in it and take a taste?"

"My finger?" Sheridan tilted his head. "Isn't that bad manners?"

Rory grinned broadly, fighting down a chuckle. "Oh, my sweet, thoughtful mate." He was so full of surprises. "The only other person here is me." Winking, Rory added huskily, "And I just had my tongue in yer mouth."

Even as Sheridan's cheeks pinked — gorgeous — he took the bowl and slid his fingertip around the edge. After tasting it, he hummed. Then he set the bowl down and grabbed the mayonnaise jar.

Loving that Sheridan was taking the initiative to make it the way he liked it, Rory turned back to the oven. He set out a hot pad and a couple of large plates. Then he opened the door again.

Rory pulled the fry tray out and set it on the hot pad. Picking up each plate, he placed one of the single-serving pepperoni French bread pizza on them in turn. With that done, he picked up the cardboard the chicken pizza had originally come on and carefully slid the pie back onto it.

Once Rory had everything out and on the counter, he shut off the oven. He swept his gaze over the spread and hummed appreciatively. His stomach even gave a soft gurgle of anticipation.

Sheridan's belly, however, once again rumbled loudly. Evidently, the ice cream had barely taken the edge off.

That's good. That means he'll enjoy this.

Rory grabbed the chef's knife out of the butcher block and turned. Spotting Spencer's look of amazement, he felt a smug satisfaction flood him. His mate's expression also held anticipation, and he loved it.

Hell yeah. I'm making my mate happy.

"Pile on as many fries as ye want, handsome," Rory encouraged as he stopped before the chicken pizza. "Or just grab the entire tray and the fry sauce. I'll get our plates and this pizza after I cut it."

"Okay," Sheridan agreed.

"Don't burn yerself," Rory cautioned when his mate reached for the tray.

Sheridan paused. "Right." He grabbed Rory's discarded oven mitt and slipped it on. "Oh, is there a corkscrew around here?" he asked as he picked up the bowl in his other hand and headed toward the fire. As he placed everything on the nearby coffee table, Sheridan continued, "I assume you want a beer?"

"That I do," Rory confirmed. He grimaced as he realized he'd never offered his mate a drink. "Sorry for being a bad host, handsome."

Shrugging one shoulder, Sheridan crossed to the front door and grabbed the twelve-pack of beer and a bottle of wine.

"Only one of us has to remember." He set the stuff down, then straightened and rested his hands on his too-slender hips. "You said shifters like to take care of their mates, that it's hard-wired into them."

It wasn't a question, but Rory nodded anyway.

With a tilt of his head, Sheridan asked, "Does that mean I'm not supposed to be able to take care of you?"

Rory's heart fluttered in his chest. Unable to help himself, he grinned extra-wide as he replied, "Oh, sweet mate. I love that ye want to take care of me." Holding up the corkscrew, he added, "Any time ye want."

When Sheridan reached for it, Rory pulled it away.

Sheridan's brows lifted in silent question.

"Kiss, please," Rory encouraged before puckering his lips.

After letting out a snicker, Sheridan obeyed.

CHAPTER NINE

Sheridan groaned as he sprawled on the bearskin rug. Rubbing his hand over his belly, he tried to keep his eyes open, but he'd damn near put himself into a food coma. Everything had tasted so good that he hadn't been able to convince himself to stop.

Chuckling softly, Rory lounged next to him. His back was against the coffee table. He had one leg bent up and the other sprawled off toward Sheridan's feet.

"Eat too much, baby?"

Frowning at Rory's teasing, Sheridan growled softly. "Not funny. Why did you let me keep crunching down the fries? And that last piece of chicken pizza." He sighed, remembering the taste. *So good.* "And that French bread pepperoni. Oh god!"

Reaching forward, Rory took Sheridan's hand and threaded their fingers together. "I didn't stop ye from eating for two reasons, my mate."

Sheridan peeled open eyelids he didn't remember closing and turned his head to stare at the bigger man. "Why?"

"Well, first," Rory began, smirking. "I'm yer mate, not yer dad. I'm never gonna stop ye from eating or drinking something unless I know it will cause ye harm." He winked before adding with a sigh, "And gods, ye looked so damn happy eating bite after bite of food that I provided, I cooked. Made me feel so damn good knowing that ye were enjoying yerself so thoroughly."

Sheridan understood. Well, he thought he did anyway. It

had to do with Rory's shifter nature.

In truth, he couldn't say he minded. Not really.

Then a jaw-cracking yawn overtook Sheridan. He lifted his free hand and covered his mouth. Once it subsided, he refocused on Rory.

"Sorry."

Rory shook his head as a smile curved up the corners of his lips. "Don't be. Ye've had a very long, very stressful day." Squeezing his hand, he murmured, "And it's definitely time for bed."

Sheridan didn't think he had the energy to go far. Managing to lift his head, he peered around the cabin. There were two doors. Both were closed.

"Um, is one a bedroom and one the john?" Sheridan hazarded.

"Yes, my mate," Rory confirmed. He pointed to the left, then the right. "Bedroom. John." Then Rory smiled at him. "We're not using the bedroom this evening. It's too cold to try to heat the entire cabin." Wincing, he added, "We'll piss fast and brush our teeth in the kitchen sink."

Understanding, Sheridan nodded. "Okay." He forced himself to a sitting position. Grabbing his glass of wine, he finished the last sip in it. "Geez, did I seriously drink the entire bottle myself?"

"Ye did." Rory winked. "I'll get ye a glass of water to guzzle real quick."

Sheridan groaned at the prospect of forcing even more of anything into him—even water. Still, he nodded. He didn't want to wake up hungover.

"Stay there and relax, Sher," Rory urged as he released him and pushed to his feet. "I need to prep a few more things for the evening." Then he crossed to the kitchen and filled a glass with water before bringing it back to him. "Here."

Taking it, Sheridan took a swallow.

Watching Rory stomp into his boots and pull on his heavy coat, Sheridan glanced around the room. Their food dishes were still scattered over the coffee table. His empty wine bottle was there, too, as were at least seven beer cans.

As soon as Rory left out the back door, Sheridan forced himself to his feet. He swayed for a second, his head swimming, but after a few blinks, his vision cleared. Crossing to the coffee table, Sheridan began collecting dishes, stacking everything on the oily cookie sheet.

Sheridan had placed it all on the counter when he heard the back door slam closed. Stepping backward, he moved out of Rory's way as he came clomping in with an armful of firewood. He swept his gaze over him and the counter, his eyebrows furrowing.

Instead of chastising Sheridan, however, Rory smiled. "I would have done that, my mate, but thank ye. Leave the dishes in the sink, and we'll take care of them in the morning." He tipped his chin toward the beer box. "If ye wanna stick the last few beers on the counter under the clock, ye can reload the box with the empties."

Pleased to have a way to help—and that Rory understood his need—Sheridan got to work. He put the empty-can-filled box in the mud-room near the garbage can and the wine bottle in it. After putting the dishes in the sink, he took a cloth and wiped down the coffee table and counters. Then Sheridan rinsed it and hung it over a dish in the sink.

Finally, Sheridan grabbed his water and sipped it. He also got out his toothbrush and paste as well as a pair of sweatpants and a long-sleeved shirt he could sleep in. Sheridan figured he would need it for warmth, even with the fire.

By then, Rory had returned with a second load of firewood. "Where are you getting that, and why does it look damp, but not snow-covered?" he asked curiously as he stood out of the way.

"We have a good-sized woodshed about twenty yards out the back door," Rory told him with a smile. "All my brothers and sisters help fill it over the summer." Waving his hand, Rory told him, "We're in the woods, so there's always plenty of deadfall or dying trees that need to be removed or culled."

Sheridan nodded.

That made sense.

"I'll step into the bathroom and change."

Sheridan didn't relish the idea of getting naked in there, since Rory had made it sound like it was pretty cold beyond that door. Still, he wasn't brave enough to change in front of the other man.

Rory shook his head. "Why don't ye change in the mud-room? Much warmer." He pointed to the bathroom. "While I take a minute in there." Smirking, Rory winked. "Will sixty seconds be enough?"

Relief filling Sheridan, he nodded. "More than."

"Grand."

Rory headed that way, so Sheridan moved to the mud-room. As he heard Rory start to whistle, perhaps to drown out the sound of him peeing, although he didn't strike Sheridan as the shy type, he began to strip. With the chilly air spurring him on, Sheridan was done in plenty of time.

Sheridan left his dirty clothes in the nearly empty hamper with his socks. Then he brushed his teeth in the kitchen sink. By the time Rory exited the bathroom, Sheridan had returned to the fire.

"It's all yers," Rory told him. Instead of heading toward the fire or the mud-room, he took a right and headed into the bed-room.

Shrugging, Sheridan hurried into the bathroom. The space was small but neat, containing a tub-shower combo, a toilet, and a pedestal sink. There was even a medicine cabinet with a mirror over it.

It was also damn cold in there.

Sheridan pushed down the front of his sweats and let out a breath even as a shiver racked his body. It took him a second to convince his cold-shriveled balls to unclench. With a sigh, he relieved his bladder.

Once done with that, Sheridan ended up pleasantly surprised to enjoy hot water to wash his hands. After drying them, he hurried back out of the room, all the while praying he didn't have to pee in the middle of the night.

That would suck.

Sheridan exited the bathroom, closing the door behind him, and froze. He couldn't help the way his brows shot up his forehead. Right before the fire, on top of the bearskin rug, was a mattress.

Rory had pushed the sofas aside to make room. He'd also spread several blankets over it. Straightening, he smiled and lifted a hand.

"I know it's a little presumptuous, but it's cold, my mate." Rory urged him closer. "Please allow me to keep ye warm tonight."

In truth, Sheridan had thought they would both sleep on the faded sofas. Rory obviously had other ideas. The man had even already changed into cut-off shorts, and he hadn't bothered with any other clothing.

Maybe he expects me to keep him warm, too.

As Sheridan slowly crossed to the fire, he couldn't help blurting out, "Aren't you going to be cold?"

Rory shook his head, his smile still in place. "No. A shifter has a much higher tolerance for hot and cold. I'll be fine." His tone however, made it seem as if he was very pleased Sheridan had asked.

Bet he thinks I'm worried about him.

Guess I am a little, too.

Once Sheridan reached Rory and took his hand, his uncertainty eased. "There's three blankets here," Rory told him.

"Climb under two and leave the third on the mattress to sleep on. It's a soft one. Very comfortable."

Sheridan nodded and obeyed. As he began to get comfortable—and the blankets were definitely very plush—Rory crossed to the table. He picked up the oil lamp and brought it over, placing it on the coffee table.

Rory offered a quick tutorial on how to light it, just in case Sheridan needed it in the night. Then he offered, "Or just wake me. I won't mind at all."

After Sheridan murmured, "Okay," Rory blew out the lamp.

Before climbing onto the mattress with him, Rory added one more log and shifted things around in the grate.

Easing close to him, Rory wrapped his arm around his waist. He positioned his front to Sheridan's back. After a kiss to his nape, Rory murmured, "Good night, my mate. Thank ye for being here with me."

Sheridan froze, his brain stalling. Then he smiled and murmured, "I'm happy to be here, Rory."

Having never slept with anyone before, Sheridan thought he would struggle to fall asleep. That wasn't the case, however. The events of the past couple of days, coupled with the epic meal and wine, caught up with him swiftly.

Wow. Only known Rory a couple of days.

That was Sheridan's last thought before sleep took him.

Sheridan woke comfortable, warm, and cozy.

Sighing, Sheridan lifted his arm to stretch . . . but he couldn't. His arm was held down by something. Confused, thinking he was tangled in his blankets, Sheridan blinked open his eyelids sleepily.

Taking in the low-burning, flickering flames in the fireplace, the events of the last few days came rushing back.

"Easy, my mate," Rory crooned, nuzzling his lips against the back of his neck. "Ye're okay. We're safe."

Slowly, Sheridan's tension eased from his body. Rory tracing his big palm down his torso helped. It also stirred up something else in him, too.

Each time Rory's fingertips reached Sheridan's belly button, only to move back up to his collarbone and start downward again, Sheridan had to bite back a whimper of need. His cock strained against the cotton of his briefs. He felt the dampness from his pre-cum and feared he'd formed a wet spot even through the sweats.

Sheridan just couldn't do anything about it. As much as he knew he should pull away, he relished the gentle caresses too much. He didn't want them to stop — not ever.

"Oh, Sheridan. My mate," Rory rumbled into his ear. "Ye do smell so nice — hungry with need and warm from the fire. Exquisite."

That caught Sheridan's attention. "You can smell, um, what?"

Rory licked a line up his neck, causing the hairs to stand on end. "A shifter has a better-than-average sense of smell," he whispered into his ear before suckling the lobe lightly.

A wave of tingles danced across Sheridan's neck, spreading across his torso. "Ror!" he whined. His nipples beaded, and his hips jerked spastically. That was when he felt it against his ass. "Oh!"

He's just as hard as I am!

"Yes, my mate," Rory murmured into his ear. "Ye do this to me without even trying." Groaning softly, he heaved a soft sigh. "If ye're not ready to share pleasure with me, I need ye to tell me now. I—" Rory moaned again, this time against his flesh as he rubbed his lips against Sheridan's neck. "I want nothing more than to please you."

Sheridan's breath caught in his chest.

What do I want?

While his first impulse was to say no, to pull away, to ask for more time, Sheridan knew that was fear talking. He didn't want to be afraid anymore. In fact, he loved everything Rory was offering him—pleasure, companionship, a relationship of equals.

In Sheridan's mind, it was beyond perfect.

"I want you," Sheridan admitted. Peering over his shoulder so he could see Rory's face, he admitted, "But I have no idea what to do."

Rory's features went from sleepy and hungry to feral and knowing. He lifted onto his elbow and peered down at him. His green eyes almost appeared to glow in his face.

Threading his fingers through Sheridan's hair, Rory told him, "It is my greatest pleasure to show ye as much pleasure as ye can handle." Then he waggled his brows as he narrowed his eyes. "And in some cases, ye may even pass out from it."

Scoffing, Sheridan shook his head. "I'm pretty sure that only happens in books."

"A challenge!" A teasing glint entered Rory's green eyes. "Excellent." He winked. Then his expression sobered a little. "Please know, if I ever do anything ye don't like, tell me. I will stop." Massaging Sheridan's scalp, Rory purred, "I only ever want to give ye pleasure."

Sheridan snickered, feeling more at peace than he'd ever thought possible . . . especially after everything that had happened.

God. Only two days.

Shaking his head, Sheridan cleared it of those thoughts. His brother and his damn issues were in the past.

"Sher?" Rory murmured. "Ye okay? Ye change yer mind?" Scraping lightly at his jaw, he smiled at him. "Know that whatever yer timing is, I can wait."

Sheridan didn't want to wait. He wanted a life. He wanted a lover.

And I want it now.

Rolling a little, Sheridan turned himself to face Rory. He

brought his hands up between them. For the first time, he initiated contact, resting his palms on Rory's pectorals.

Oh wow! Ripped!

Sheridan had always been on the slender side, but not so with Rory. As he skimmed his palms over the man, a shiver of desire caused his gut to clench. His already engorged dick throbbed.

As Sheridan touched his lightly haired chest, Rory let out a deep groan. The sound seemed to vibrate right up his arms, and his breath caught in his chest. Lifting his gaze to Rory, he finally understood the phrase—*looked at him with fire in his eyes.*

Rory's deep green eyes appeared to glow.

"Wow," Sheridan mumbled, anticipation setting his blood on fire. "Now what?"

"Now," Rory rumbled, tightening his arm around his waist. "I'm going to make out with ye, rock against ye, strip ye, and make ye come." His smile turned feral. "Then I'm gonna lick ye clean with my tongue and suck ye back to hardness while I open yer ass before sinkin' into ye and claimin' ye for my own."

Sheridan couldn't help the shudder that worked through him. "Yes, please."

CHAPTER TEN

Rory's heart soared as he heard Sheridan's whimpers. His body vibrated in his arms. Even the way he stared up at him with his big, hazel eyes set Rory's blood on fire.

My mate wants me.

With that thought in mind, Rory vowed to give Sheridan the most blissful cherry-popping experience of his life. He never wanted his mate to second-guess himself. The man in his arms was his end all and be all for the rest of his centuries-long life . . . and Rory couldn't wait to get started.

First, Rory needed to fulfill his promise.

Kissing and frotting.

Rory dipped his head and nuzzled his lips along Sheridan's jaw. Enjoying the scrape of the light five o'clock shadow against his lips, he worked his way to Sheridan's ear. As he suckled the delicate flap, he felt his mate's panting breaths sending warm gusts across his ear.

His cock jerked in response, and he smiled around the bit of flesh he worked.

As Rory distracted Sheridan, he slid a hand under his shirt. He could feel every rib under his smooth skin and made a mental note to feed up his mate. If his man's natural body type was skinny, that was fine, but Rory needed to be sure.

Pushing that instinct to the back burner, Rory focused on other desires — giving his mate as much bliss as possible. He worked his lips down Sheridan's jaw to his lips. Capturing them fully, he thrust his tongue deep.

Rory groaned upon tasting his mate's natural flavors, even

mixed a little with stale wine and morning breath. None of that mattered as he felt Sheridan kiss him back, his tongue sliding experimentally against his own. Using his own appendage to encourage the tongue-play, Rory rubbed his palm under his shirt, teasing the smooth, hairless flesh.

His cock throbbed insistently. The skin of his palm almost felt on fire as he touched his mate's flesh. His heart hammered in his chest as he continued to ease Sheridan's shirt upward.

Once there was no way around it, Rory broke the kiss. He gripped the hem of Sheridan's shirt and tugged up. "Off," he encouraged.

To Rory's smug satisfaction, Sheridan didn't even hesitate. As soon as the fabric cleared his mate's body, Rory rolled on top of him, pressing him into the mattress. The blanket slipped, but he easily grabbed it and pulled it back over them.

Don't want my mate to get cold.

At the same time, Rory captured Sheridan's mouth in another feral kiss. He rocked his hips, grinding his groin against his new lover's.

Don't give a shit about what others decide is a lover. He's mine.

As Rory continued to kiss Sheridan, worshiping his mouth with lips and tongue, occasionally parting their lips so they could both suck in much-needed lungfuls of air, he mapped his torso with the fingers of his right hand. When he reached Sheridan's sweatpants, he dipped his fingertips beneath the band. Rory scraped his nails ever-so-lightly over the skin covering the groove of his hip.

Turning his head, Sheridan broke the kiss. He groaned wantonly as he shuddered beneath him. His hands gripped Rory's biceps as little mewls escaped his mouth.

All the while, Sheridan ground against Rory.

Rory's smug pride swelled within him, but he wanted more. For one heartbeat, two, he lifted his hips just a little. He shoved his own sweat shorts down, releasing his cock and balls. Then he grabbed the front of Sheridan's sweatpants and pulled them up and down, too, taking his briefs with them.

Because Sheridan probably hadn't been expecting it, he didn't lift his hips. That was okay, though. With Rory's shifter strength, he made it work, getting the fabric low enough to tuck beneath his mate's groin.

Just as Sheridan began to whine with confusion and need, Rory lowered his hips once again. He pressed his hard-on against his mate's and rocked his hips. Hearing the swift inhale followed by the keening cry of pleasure was the best damn music to Rory's ears.

It took one rut, two, before Rory felt hot seed spilling all over his groin and stomach. Sheridan cried out, the sound of ecstasy bouncing off the walls, causing his balls to tingle. Even the way Sheridan's nails dug into his skin didn't stop the rising wave of his orgasm. In fact, it intensified it.

"Yesss," Rory rumbled, unable to help himself. "Love to wear yer marks."

Then Rory's balls felt as if they turned inside out. His shaft jerked and throbbed. Even his neck arched as he cried out his mate's name to the rafters.

Coming back to himself who knew how long later, Rory felt relief that he hadn't crushed his smaller mate. Somehow, he still rested most of his weight on his left arm. He had his head tucked against Sheridan's neck, and he was absently mouthing sucking kisses against the flesh.

The gums around his canines tingled, but his teeth hadn't extended, yet.

Sighing deeply, Rory lifted his head. He smiled upon seeing the blissed-out expression on Sheridan's face. His eyes were closed, his lips were parted, and his cheeks were flushed. Even the sweat gleaming on his brow was a thing of beauty.

Rory couldn't help himself. He leaned forward and swiped

his tongue across his mate's brow. The man's salty-sweet flavor burst across his taste buds.

Sheridan's lips twitched, and he cracked his eyelids. "Wow," he mumbled. He rubbed his hands up and down Rory's arms and shoulders. "Amazing."

"Ye ain't seen nothin' yet," Rory crooned thickly, his desire for his mate quickly rising.

Rory had no clue how Brennan had managed to stay away from Wilson for months. He'd only known Sheridan a couple of days, and he felt as if he would go out of his damn mind if he couldn't keep touching and exploring him. Of course, at the time, Brennan hadn't actually known who Wilson was or where to find him.

Pushing those thoughts aside, Rory focused on what was important—driving Sheridan out of his ever-loving mind.

With that goal in mind, Rory pecked a kiss to Sheridan's lips. Then he started working down his lover, licking along his collarbone, sipping at the hollow of his neck, and suckling lightly on his Adam's apple. He took the blanket with him as he worked his way to Sheridan's nipple, wanting to see his mate's gorgeous flushed skin and trusting that the lingering fire and arousal would keep him warm.

Sheridan panted, his chest rising and falling rapidly as Rory licked and laved around his taut bud. When he scraped his tongue over the peak, Sheridan whimpered beautifully. The noise he made when Rory wrapped his lips around the nub and sucked was even better—a moan while he arched, pressing into his touch.

Loving that response, Rory continued to suck at his nipple for another moment. Then he slid his lips across his chest to his other bud, cleaning any seed he found along the way. Rory gave Sheridan's other nip the same treatment, enjoying his cries of pleasure. At the same time, he wriggled his hips a little and kicked off his sweat shorts.

Rory flicked his gaze upward, taking in Sheridan's expression. His flushed face sported slightly curved lips and a glazed expression. Sweat gleamed on his brows, and his fingers were twisted in the blanket beneath him.

His slender neck was arched, leading to a lean torso. No chest hair covered his frame, but lean muscles slid under the skin of his arms. As Rory moved his lips downward, he admired Sheridan's almost too-thin frame as he licked along the lines of his ribs.

"My beautiful mate," Rory murmured as he nosed over the groove of his hip. "Stunning."

Sheridan groaned softly, his hips shifting restlessly. "Y-You're the b-beautiful one," he managed to rasp between panting breaths.

Rory flashed his mate a pleased smile. "So glad ye think so."

While Rory had never considered himself a vain man, he knew plenty of people found him good-looking. All their opinions didn't matter, though. Only Sheridan's did.

"May I take these off of ye, Sher?" Rory asked, rising up a little so he could get a better grip on the waistband of Sheridan's sweats and underwear. "Can I see all of ye?"

Upon seeing the beautiful maybe seven-inch shaft jutting from Sheridan's thin patch of dark-blond pubes, Rory swallowed. His watering mouth immediately filled again. He wanted to taste that lovely piece of meat so badly.

"O-Okay," Sheridan whispered.

While Sheridan sounded uncertain, his scent screamed his need. He also lifted his hips.

Rory took no time in pulling Sheridan free of his clothing. He even paused long enough to slide his mate's socks off. Once Rory knelt between his naked human's spread calves, he groaned and gripped the base of his once-again throbbing shaft.

"Oh, Sheridan," Rory said on a groan.

Sheridan smiled up at him, his hazel eyes darkening to an amber color. "Like the way you look at me," he admitted. Untwisting his fingers from the blanket, he slid the tips of one hand up his hip. "The way you touch me."

Growling, Rory gave his mate a feral grin. "I'll do more than touch ye, my mate." As he moved back over Sheridan and nuzzled his chin into the groove on his mate's other hip, he muttered, "Gonna make ye feel so good."

"Yessss," Sheridan hissed, his hands coming to rest on Rory's shoulders.

Sheridan didn't push or pull. He didn't try to guide Rory, although he would have been happy to take direction from his mate. Rory figured his human just needed the connection. Plus, with his lack of experience, he probably didn't know what he wanted or needed, anyway.

Gonna change all that.

Rory set to work. He balanced on his knees, so he could rub and massage Sheridan's thighs with his hands. Following that up with licking the sensitive nerve endings of his inner thigh, Rory worked his way down one leg.

Teasing and nipping at the back of Sheridan's knee drew a harsh noise from his human's lips—a cross between a groan and a laugh. When he worked his thumbs into the arch of his foot, his mate moaned. Sucking on his toes yanked a squeak from the man, and he tried to pull away.

Letting go of his foot, Rory grinned up at Sheridan. "Is that a no?"

Sheridan snickered even as he stared at him with wide eyes. "Um . . . not this time?"

Even though Sheridan sounded confused, Rory nodded as he gripped his human's other foot and began a short massage. Seeing if his mate enjoyed toe play could be revisited. It wasn't for everyone, especially a virgin. Personally, he could take it or leave it, but he wanted to discover and fulfill all of

Sheridan's desires.

As Rory worked up Sheridan's other leg, his mate huffed and moaned, lying back down. His other leg shifted restlessly as soft grunts escaped his parted lips. When Rory's nose bumped into Sheridan's balls, he whimpered.

"Gods, I love the noises ye make," Rory mumbled before he began mouthing the skin of his sack.

"R-Rory!" Sheridan cried, undulating beneath him.

Rory grinned against his flesh, knowing what his mate was actually asking for. More than happy to suck Sheridan's dick, he licked up the underside of his shaft. Once he reached the tip, he wrapped his lips around his crown and swiped over his leaking slit.

Sheridan let out a deep hiss, so Rory did it again.

At the same time, Rory reached over and slid his hand under the side of the mattress. He began sinking deeper and deeper onto his lover's shaft, enjoying the rich flavor of his erection. After a second, he found what he wanted and pulled out a tube of lubricant.

He'd shoved it there while making up the bed the previous evening. It'd been wishful thinking, but he'd hoped. Now he was glad he'd been so prepared.

As Rory picked up his ministrations to Sheridan's cock, sucking and massaging, he used a thumb to pop the lube's cap. Then he poured a liberal dollop onto the fingers of his left hand. After closing it and setting it aside, Rory slid his right hand under Sheridan's thigh and eased it to the side, opening his mate further.

Rory lowered his head, taking Sheridan to the root. Pausing there, he swallowed around his mate's crown. At the same time, he tipped his head down a little, sliding the thin hair of his goatee over Sheridan's groin.

Sheridan's cry of delighted surprise echoed over the cabin walls.

Smiling around his mouthful, Rory began to suck up again. He breathed noisily through his nose as he began teasing behind Sheridan's balls with his lubed fingertips. When Rory glided over his mate's hole, he felt the man tense, so he didn't push in.

Instead, Rory began a slow sucking bobbing on Sheridan's prick. At the same time, he continued to massage over and around his hole, getting him used to the touch. He rubbed his right hand up, plucking at a nipple.

To Rory's pleasure, he felt Sheridan's striated muscle relax while other parts of him tightened. His stomach clenched, and he began rocking into Rory's mouth. He didn't stop him. Instead, he used the momentum.

After the first several rocks, Rory positioned his digit at Sheridan's entrance. He used his mate's own rutting to breach his muscle. His finger sank halfway into his lover.

Sheridan groaned, but the rocking of his hips never slowed.

Rory used that to his advantage. Each time Sheridan bobbed up, he eased his finger partway out. On the move down, he pushed it deeper. Soon, he was finger-fucking his mate with ease, so he began working a second digit into him.

Moaning, Sheridan's hips stuttered, then stopped. He panted and whined. "I-I-I—"

Rubbing over Sheridan's stomach, Rory lifted from his mate's prick. "Easy, my mate," he crooned, petting his human. "Keep breathing."

It was so damn hard to keep his fingers still. He wanted to push in and stretch his mate. His cock throbbed with each beat of his heart, ramping up his desire to mount and claim. His wolf's mental urgings to take their mate didn't help much, either.

Fighting back his instincts, Rory smiled reassuringly at Sheridan. "Ye're just fine, Sher," he murmured, taking in his flushed face and taut features. "We can wait if ye're not ready for me to claim ye."

Sheridan met his gaze with wide eyes. His short blond hair stuck to his temples, and his pupils were dilated. His bottom lip looked a little red, probably from where he'd been nibbling it.

"Gods, ye look like a debauched angel," Rory muttered. "So fuckin' sexy."

A wide smile slowly curved Sheridan's lips. He stared up at him with a gleam in his hazel eyes that caused Rory's heart to skip a beat. Then he let out a long sigh, and Rory felt the instant loosening around his two fingers.

"I want this, Rory," Sheridan assured. "I want you." He rocked his hips up and down, slowly fucking himself on Rory's digits. "Please, I want to finish what we started."

Letting out a deep groan, Rory nodded. "Anything for you, Sheridan." Then he leaned over his groin again. "Just remember to stay as relaxed as ye can. I gotta add another finger first."

After receiving a nod from Sheridan, Rory swallowed his mate's prick to the root. At the same time, he crooked his fingers. Hearing his mate's cry of bliss, he smiled around the man's dick.

Found his prostate. Sweet.

CHAPTER ELEVEN

When Sheridan had first felt Rory's finger in his ass, he hadn't given it much thought. He knew the man would need to fuck him. The discomfort had been mild, easily drowned out by the pleasure Rory was creating by sucking his cock.

That changed when Rory worked his second finger into him. The burning stretch had been so intense. He'd wondered why the fuck men did this, and he'd frozen.

Then, seeing Rory's understanding expression, hearing his words of reassurance and patience, something in Sheridan had relaxed. He'd wanted what Rory was offering. That meant dealing with the pain.

After all, Rory had experienced plenty of pain in his life, and this would be fleeting with a great reward at the end.

Except, then Rory had touched something deep inside him. It set his nerve endings on fire, causing his cock to twitch. His channel felt as if it had been lit up, and the skin of his groin goose bumped.

Sheridan even felt his balls begin to tighten.

Grabbing one of Rory's shoulders, Sheridan tugged his long dark hair lightly with the other. "R-Rory!" he whined, trying to find words to warn the man. "G-Gon-Gonna—"

Even though Sheridan had been trying to warn Rory, when the man popped off his cock, he whined with dismay.

"Then come, my sweet Sheridan," Rory urged, nuzzling his goatee up and down the sensitive skin of his length. "Fill my mouth with your cream."

Rory once again swallowed his dick to the root.

Sheridan groaned and shuddered. His erection throbbed, and his balls tightened. He snapped his hips up once, twice, losing control of his body.

When Sheridan's release bowled through him, his senses soared. Spots danced across his vision. He even forgot to breathe as his orgasm forced pulse after pulse of cum up his dick. Rory swallowed his seed as he continued to suck, extending the bliss-inducing sensations coursing through him.

Vacantly, Sheridan felt Rory ease his fingers out of him. He rubbed over that ecstasy-giving pleasure nub as he did so. Humming, Sheridan didn't fight it when Rory rolled him to his side, facing the fire.

Rory lifted his left leg, positioning a pillow under it. Then he slotted up behind him, sliding his right arm under his body. He curved his arm up, clutching him to Rory's chest.

Sheridan sighed heavily, pressing into Rory's warm, gentle hold.

The sting to his chute didn't register at first. His brain had been completely fuzzed-out. The increase of the burn finally caught his attention, and he realized Rory was sinking his erection deep into him.

"Relax, Sheridan, my mate," Rory urged before sucking on his neck. He brought his left arm around and teased over his hip before skimming his fingertips around his still-half-hard prick. "Push out and let me in, my love."

While it sounded completely counter-intuitive to Sheridan, he trusted the man behind him. He did as he'd been told. Pushing out, he discovered it did make it easier, and soon, he felt Rory's groin hair rubbing against his ass cheeks.

"Oh, Sheridan," Rory moaned into his ear. "Thank ye so much. So good. So hot and tight."

Rory's right arm tightened even as he continued to play with his nipple. With his left hand, he skimmed up and down

Sheridan's prick, encouraging it to fill again. He even fondled his balls, teasing over the sensitive skin of his sack.

Sheridan trembled in Rory's arms, the mixture of tingles, zings, and fire causing a riot on his senses. Except . . . he felt like something was missing. He needed . . . something.

A shiver worked through Sheridan, and the skin of his arms goose bumped. "Rory? I—" Sheridan didn't know how to express something he didn't understand.

"I know what ye need, Sher," Rory claimed. "I was just waitin' for ye to relax enough to enjoy it."

Sheridan nodded, even as confusion continued to fill him. Then Rory began to move his hips, and everything became clear. Rory's thick erection caressed his inner walls, sliding along the sensitive nerves there. His crown slid over his hot spot, crashing blissful zings through his body once more.

"Gods, I love the sounds ye make," Rory moaned into his ear as he drove his dick into him over and over. "So beautiful. Sets my body on fire."

Sheridan would have asked what he meant, but he was too busy letting out a litany of groans, grunts, and whimpers. He grabbed Rory's left wrist with his own and twisted his right hand into the blanket. Using the hold for leverage, he began pushing into each of Rory's ruts.

The pleasure of having Rory's dick sliding in and out of him swiftly went to Sheridan's head. He knew he would want to feel this over and over, as often as possible. The man's cock felt exquisite inside him, setting his body on fire in ways he'd never dreamed.

To Sheridan's shock, his cock once again leaked and twitched. He gritted his teeth, chasing that feeling. His balls rolled and tightened, and he knew he was getting close.

"Come, baby," Rory urged into his ear. "Come for me again."

Sheridan wasn't certain he could obey. He didn't know if

he was close enough . . . especially having already come twice. Then he felt Rory cup his ball sack and give it a massaging roll.

Gasping, Sheridan felt his testicles pull tight. His release burst through his body. He shouted Rory's name as ecstasy sang through him, and he painted the blanket before him.

Black and white spots danced across his vision, but he still registered the heat that suddenly filled his chute. He felt the twitch of Rory's dick inside his body. The roar of pleasure bursting from the man behind him caused him to grin smugly.

I pleased my man. My shifter.

Then Rory clamped his mouth on the point of Sheridan's shoulder. He hummed, thinking the man was going to suck and kiss his neck some more. When pain stabbed through his flesh, he opened his mouth with a gasp . . . which he immediately let out on a cry of pleasure.

Unable to fight it, Sheridan felt his eyes roll to the back of his head when the bliss crashed over his senses again.

The soft licking and nuzzling to his neck drew Sheridan slowly back to consciousness. He cracked open his eyelids, then blinked them several times to get his vision to clear. His gaze fell on a roaring fire, and he smiled.

Then Sheridan felt the arm around his waist and the hot body slotted up behind his own naked one.

Hot damn. I just lost my virginity.

Sheridan couldn't help it. A giggle escaped him. Biting his bottom lip, he cut off the unmanly noise.

"Hmmm," Rory hummed from behind him as he rubbed his nose against the back of his neck. "Now there's a pleasant sound."

Rory's voice came out husky and low, even a little raspy. The sound caused Sheridan's gut to clench pleasantly. Tipping his head forward, he encouraged the other man's gentle touches.

"Yeah?" Sheridan couldn't help but point out, "Giggles aren't very manly."

Growling softly, Rory tightened his hold. "Who gives a fuck." Then he licked another line over Sheridan's skin. "The noise means ye're happy. I like makin' ye happy." Rory suckled on one of the knobs at the back of his neck. "Ye taste so damn good when ye're happy."

"I taste different?" Sheridan had to turn his head, so he could meet his lover's eyes.

Hot damn. I have a lover!

"Mmm-hmmm," Rory confirmed. "Exquisite."

Then Rory pressed his lips to Sheridan's. He drew away much too soon, but only so he could urge him to roll onto his back. Levering over him, Rory slung his leg over Sheridan's, then dove back in for another make-out session.

After so many orgasms, Sheridan didn't expect his dick to be able to harden again, but his prick certainly gave it the old college try. He was half-hard when Rory lifted his head. With a smile curving his kiss-plumped lips, he rested his head on his hand and peered down at him.

"How are ye feeling, sweetheart?" Rory asked. "I didn't miss any cum bits, did I?"

"You cleaned me?" Surprise filled Sheridan as Rory nodded. Although, it made sense, because he didn't feel sticky from seed or slick. "How long was I out?"

Rory grinned. "Maybe ten minutes. Long enough for me to toss a few logs on the fire and stoke it up. Take a piss, brush my teeth, pre-heat the oven, and clean ye up." He winked. "Cinnamon rolls should be ready in ten."

Sheridan laughed. "Wow. You got a lot done!" It was then he noticed smells other than wood smoke that permeated the cabin.

"I did, didn't I?" Rory looked extremely pleased with himself. "Did ye want any coffee?"

Sheridan shook his head. "No thanks. I prefer juice."

"Ah, the grapefruit juice ye picked out," Rory replied with a nod. "Are ye ready for some?"

As Rory spoke, Sheridan's stomach growled. He felt his face heat a little, this time not from arousal. Rory just laughed before pecking a kiss to his lips.

"Stay here and keep warm. I'll be right back."

Sheridan would have obeyed, but his bladder took that moment to twinge. "Uh, actually, gonna hit the head."

Rory nodded. "Okay."

Jumping to his feet, Sheridan rushed to the bathroom. He heard Rory's chuckles and paused in the doorway. It was then he recalled that he was still naked, and he'd just flashed his ass at the man.

Sheridan would have felt self-conscious, but then he saw the expression on Rory's face. His lover was raking him with the hottest look of appreciation that he'd ever seen. Rory even paused at his package and licked his lips.

With his heart thudding swiftly for a new reason, Sheridan snickered before closing the bathroom door.

After taking care of his morning business, Sheridan exited the room. He sighed as the warmth filling the main cabin wrapped around him. As he began closing the door, Rory shook his head.

"Leave it open, love," Rory encouraged. "We'll get the room heated a little today. I'm certain ye'll appreciate a shower later." With a wink, he added, "I hate getting out of hot water only to freeze my balls off."

Chuckling, Sheridan nodded. As he crossed to the kitchen, he couldn't help but check out the naked man waiting for him there. He'd never been naked around anyone before, and he had to fight back his self-consciousness . . . especially considering the sexy hunk of man before him.

Rory stood an inch or two over Sheridan's own six-foot

height. His skin was naturally bronzed with toned, defined muscles on his limbs. Not a scar marred his body, and a little black hair smattered across his chest.

His green eyes twinkled in his face, a thin goatee bracketed his mouth of sin, and his shoulder-length black hair cradled his roguish features.

"Sex on a stick."

"Excuse me?"

Realizing he'd said that out loud, he rolled his eyes. "I'm sure plenty of people have called you that."

Rory shrugged one shoulder before reaching out and cradling Sheridan's jaw. His expression grew serious. "Only yer opinion means anything to me, Sheridan."

"Wow." Sheridan swallowed hard. "I—"

Before Sheridan could say more, a scratching noise sounded in the direction of the back door.

Releasing him, Rory grumbled, "I thought I'd have more time." He smacked Sheridan's ass lightly, ordering, "Get dressed, my mate. If he sees ye naked, I'll have to cut his eyes out."

Sheridan wasn't certain who he was talking about, but he obeyed. "What about you?" he asked, figuring someone had to be at the door.

"There's a bunch of extra sweats and other clothes in the mud-room," Rory told him, heading that way. He grinned wildly and waggled his eyebrows. "It's a shifter thing, love."

As Rory nodded, his heart rate spiked in his chest. His mate had called him a lot of pet names, but damn did he love that one best. As he pulled on the sweatpants and long-sleeved shirt he'd worn to sleep, he wondered if Rory meant his words.

Sheridan didn't have the guts to ask, though.

Maybe someday.

The sound of claws on hardwood drew his attention. He'd just turned when a massive black and gray wolf padded into the room. Gasping, he took a step backward . . . and tripped on the mattress. He landed with a thump on the bedding.

Sheridan's instincts screamed at him to jump up and run to the bathroom, to lock himself somewhere safe.

"Whoa, whoa!" Suddenly, Rory was crouching beside him. "Just relax. That's my brother." Wrapping his arms around him, Rory pulled him into a tight embrace. "I shoulda warned ye. Sorry about that."

"Y-Your brother?" Sheridan peered at the wolf again even as he cuddled in Rory's hold, gripping the fresh shirt the man had put on at some point. Something he'd missed caught his attention. "With a backpack."

The canine dropped the big green duffel bag he'd been carrying in his mouth. The animal's green eyes, so similar to Rory's own, gleamed with intelligence. He chuffed softly, then padded back the way he'd come.

"Yes, my brother with a backpack," Rory confirmed as the odd sounds of snapping and popping came from the laundry room. "His name is Cullen."

Sheridan nodded slowly. "Cullen." He recognized the name. "He was there the night we met."

"Right."

"Good of ye to remember me, Sheridan," a dark-haired man commented as he exited the laundry room. "And it's good to officially meet ye." Then he pulled a shirt over his head before pausing next to the oven and opening it. "Oh, damn. Cinnamon rolls."

"Hey! Those are ours," Rory cried, jumping to his feet and rushing to the kitchen. "Get away from those."

Cullen placed both hands over his heart, sporting a wounded expression. "I brought ye clothes in a snowstorm, and ye won't even give me one?"

"Hell, no!" Rory replied, taking the tray out of the oven and placing it on the top of the stove. "And it's not a snowstorm anymore."

Shrugging, Cullen countered, "Near enough. It's still snowing pretty heavy." Then his eyes narrowed and a smirk curved his lips. "I suppose if my mouth is empty, I can tell yer mate all about yer youthful shenanigans." Cullen turned and headed toward the living room. "Back when Rory was only sixty-two, he bought his first motorcycle. He—"

"Fine!" Rory shouted. "Ye can have a coupla cinnamon rolls." He growled under his breath. "Bloody black-mailer."

Unable to help himself, Sheridan chuckled at their antics. Then he pushed up from the mattress and headed into the kitchen to retrieve the glass of grapefruit juice sitting on the counter. Rory must have poured it for him when he'd been in the bathroom.

Sheridan had just finished swallowing a mouthful when Cullen leaned close and sniffed. A wide grin curved his lips, and he pulled Sheridan into a hug.

"Welcome to the family, Sheridan."

Returning Cullen's hug, Sheridan stared over his shoulder at Rory.

His lover grinned and winked, then returned his attention to drizzling the cinnamon rolls with sugary icing.

Wow. A new family.

Sheridan's heart tripped in his chest, and something foreign flooded him.

Happiness.

CHAPTER TWELVE

R eaching over the *Bronco*'s bench seat, Rory squeezed
Sheridan's thigh. "Easy over there, Sheridan. It'll be
okay."

"Please put both hands on the wheel."

Rory obeyed, fighting the smile that twitched around the
corners of his lips. He knew his mate wouldn't appreciate his
mirth. While Rory understood what caused Sheridan's nerves
while driving on snowy roads, he knew he would get them
there safely.

Hell, the roads weren't really all that bad. The snowplows
had come through, the sun had been out most of the day, and
any ice would have melted. On top of that, he had his *Bronco*
in four-wheel-drive . . . and he was going five under the speed
limit.

Even with all those precautions, Sheridan still held the *oh
shit* handle in a white-knuckled grip. His other hand was
fisted in his lap. He stared out the windshield with wide eyes.

"Please try to relax, my love," Rory encouraged. He hated
the acrid scent of his mate's tension. "I'll get us there safely."

"Do you really?"

Confused by the question, Rory glanced Sheridan's way.
His mate's eyebrows were furrowed, and his lips were
pinched. Still, his left hand now lay flat on his thigh.

Progress.

"Do I really what?"

"Love me?"

Rory tipped his head, wondering why Sheridan would ask

that. Most humans didn't talk about love so swiftly. While it was true that he did love his mate, he hadn't planned to spring it on Sheridan until they'd been together a little longer.

His hesitation must have given Sheridan the wrong idea. "I see," he murmured with a sigh. "Just a pet name."

Sheridan muttered that last part so quietly, Rory wouldn't have heard him if he hadn't been a shifter.

Ah. I see.

"I do love you, Sheridan," Rory stated confidently, instilling his voice with calmness. "Ye're the most important person in my life until the end of our days. I love yer snark, yer sexy body, yer playfulness when ye let it out, and yer talent." Another quick look in Sheridan's direction showed his mate's wide-eyed expression as he stared at him. "I even love that ye tried to protect Kendra in yer own way, even though it meant ye occasionally ended up hurt."

Rory and Cullen had talked with Sheridan over breakfast about the situation with Spencer and Payne. Sheridan had shared how he'd refused to steal the expensive bracelet that Wilson had given his daughter when she'd worn it to their house one day. Spencer had pounded on Sheridan until he'd pissed blood for three days.

If I could raise him from the dead, I'd kill him all over again.

"Wow," Sheridan whispered. "I love you, too." He reached over and rested his hand on Rory's thigh. "Even though I think it's way too damn soon."

Chuckling softly, Rory winked at Sheridan. "I love hearing ye say that." Then he added, "And it's a shifter thing."

Sheridan snickered. "There's a lot of shifter things."

"There are," Rory confirmed, pleased that he'd helped his mate calm. "Ye'll learn them all in time." Grinning widely, he reminded, "Which we'll have plenty of."

Nodding, Sheridan sighed. "I can't believe Wilson and Kendra are meeting us at Caribou's."

That had been another bit of news Cullen had given them.

Wilson had wanted to talk to Sheridan in a neutral setting. Sheridan could have said no, but he wanted to clear the air just as much as Wilson did.

His mate had told him he didn't want to keep Rory estranged from his youngest brother.

If Rory hadn't already been in love with Sheridan by then, he would have fallen hard and fast upon hearing that.

"I admit, I'm a little surprised, too," Rory began slowly. Then he shook his head. "Ye know what. I'm actually not."

"What do you mean?"

"Well, think about it." Rory smiled as he thought about Brennan's mate. "Wilson is an advocate for homeopathic remedies and holistic healing. Holding a grudge would mess up his chi or his internal energy or whatever that shit is called." Grinning widely, Rory chuckled. "He'll want to clear the negative energy from between ye as swiftly as possible. His motives may be a little selfish, but I'm okay with that."

"Huh." Sheridan nodded slowly. "Okay. I can see that." After clearing his throat, he admitted, "I never really thought about how his shop might impact his beliefs."

"Or how his beliefs could have helped him decide on that kind of shop?"

"Yeah." Sheridan nodded again. "Yeah."

Rory rolled slowly past the welcome sign for Stone Ridge and slowed his vehicle. Spotting the sign for Caribou's, the nicest steak house in town, he flipped on his blinker. As he turned his *Bronco* into the parking lot, even in the dim lighting cast by the setting sun, Rory spotted his brother's *Jeep*.

Since they were coming into town at dusk, Rory figured Sheridan would have an even tougher time on the drive back to the cabin.

We'll cross that bridge when we come to it.

"I see Brennan's *Jeep*," Rory commented absently. "I wonder if they've already gotten us a table."

Just as Rory finished speaking the words, he spotted his

brother's form near the edge of the parking lot. He frowned as he parked. Turning off the vehicle, he saw a snowball sail through the air and hit Brennan on his thigh.

Brennan tipped his head back and laughed as he scooped up his own ball of the white stuff. Then he lobbed it back at someone.

Smirking, Rory shut off the engine, then pointed their way. "Looks like they're having a snowball fight while they waited for us."

That was when Wilson came barreling around the side of a car. He grabbed Brennan around the waist and drove him backward. With a look of joy on his face, his brother tumbled into the snowbank created by the plowed snow.

"They look like they're having fun," Sheridan commented softly.

"They do." Rory reached over and squeezed his hand. "Let's go join them. We have ten minutes before our reservation."

Even as Rory led the way out of the *Bronco*, he heard the reservation in Sheridan's tone. "Oh, I don't know." Turning to look at him, Rory saw the way he nibbled his lower lip before he added, "I don't want to intrude."

Rory scoffed as he held out his hand. "Nonsense. They're crashing our first date, so it's only fair we hit 'em with a few snowballs." After Sheridan slid his hand into Rory's own, he gave his lover a cheeky grin. "Besides, it'll be fun."

"O-Okay."

Pleased with Sheridan's acquiescence, Rory started in his brother's direction. Brennan and Wilson had just risen to their feet when he spotted a squealing Kendra pop up from around another car. She threw a snowball. While some of the poorly formed ball splintered off, a good-sized chunk managed to plop against Wilson's chest.

Rory chuckled and released Sheridan's hand. Reaching

out, he swept his fingers through the snow piled on the roof of a car they were walking past. He ignored the cold and quickly formed a ball.

Then Rory chucked it at Brennan.

His aim was true, and the orb slammed into the back of his brother's head.

With a roar, Brennan turned. He spotted them and glared, but Rory knew there was no anger in his eyes. "Oh, ye fucker! It's on!" Then Brennan bent and carved out a handful of the snowbank.

"Daddy Brennan!" Kendra cried. "You said a bad word!"

Aww, isn't that cute?

"Sorry, princess," Brennan called as he wound up. "I'll put a dollar in the swear jar when we get home." Then he zinged his ball at Rory.

For the next five minutes, the group threw snowballs at each other. Well, to be fair, Brennan and Rory pelted each other while the others were much more mild about it. Rory did appreciate that Sheridan tossed a couple, too, although he looked a little uncomfortable.

My mate is still trying.

Finally, the fighting wound down. Rory knew it was time for their reservation. They'd changed it to five people instead of two that morning after talking with Cullen.

"Everyone ready for supper?" Rory called. Then he reached out a hand and held it out to Wilson. "It's good to see ye again, Wilson."

Wilson nodded. "You, too." After they shook, his gaze strayed to Sheridan. "Sheridan."

"Hi, Wilson. I—" Sheridan rubbed at his chest. "I'm so sorry. I—"

"God, what a fucking homo-fest," a deep voice snarled as a large figure appeared from between several trees. "This is the most disgusting display I've ever seen, and I've seen some shit."

Sheridan stiffened. "Payne."

"You're in so much trouble for making me track you all the way out here, Sheridan," Payne claimed. "Where's Spencer? Where's my shit?"

"You said a bad word," Kendra said on a whisper.

"Shut up, brat," Payne snapped, glaring at the girl.

"Leave her alone," Sheridan ordered, stepping forward. "I already texted you from Spencer's phone. He's dead. I don't know what you agreed to buy from him, so I don't know where your" — he hesitated — "*stuff* is."

While Sheridan was lying about having texted Payne himself, the man *had* been sent a message from Spencer's phone . . . by Raul.

Rory watched Payne stick his hand inside his coat and pull out a handgun — a *Glock* if he didn't miss his guess.

"Sir, I'm an officer in this town," Rory began, keeping his voice level. He took a step forward with his palms raised. "This isn't going to get you what you want."

Payne smirked as he flicked his gaze Rory's way. "Sure it will. I'll even give your faggot asses a choice." His smile turned cruel. "My shit. My money." He lifted his gun and pointed it at Sheridan. "Or your life."

"That's not happening," Rory declared, easing toward his mate, trying to slip between him and Payne.

"Stop moving," Payne ordered. "One more step and I'll *make* you stop moving." He chortled. "I don't care whose life I take, but it'll be one of yours."

Rory gritted his teeth as he glanced discreetly around the area. They were too spread out. Brennan caught his eye and eased a step closer toward Payne.

"I can't give you your money back," Sheridan stated, re-drawing Payne's attention . . . and his aim. "Spencer willed everything to Shandell, so only she could refund the money."

Sheridan shook his head. "And I know she won't. She's a self-ish bitch." He glanced toward Kendra and whispered, "Sorry, sweetie. I'll give you a dollar for your swear jar later."

Kendra nodded solemnly.

"And all of his jewelry has been seized by the police," Rory told the man, hoping he would point the gun at him again. A shifter had a much better chance of recovering fully from a gunshot than a human, even a mated one.

Payne growled low in his throat, and his eyes narrowed. "Then your lives."

Before Rory could try to reason with him again, to get him to see that there was no way he would get away if he started shooting—*hell, he isn't getting away regardless, but he doesn't need to know that*—Payne swung his arm again.

"Starting with the brat," Payne declared.

"No!" Wilson screamed.

Even as Rory lunged forward, trying to get between himself and Kendra, he knew he wouldn't be quick enough. The blast of a gun going off echoed through the night air. That was followed by a feminine scream, another blast, and the snarls of a wolf.

Rory hit the ground as pain blossomed through his side. For an instant, he thought maybe he'd made it. Then the sound of a young girl crying reached his ears.

Shit!

Gritting his teeth, Rory rolled to his knees. A quick look toward Payne revealed Brennan in wolf form ravaging the man. Blood and gore stained the snowy ground as Brennan ripped the man apart.

Rory peered toward Kendra and gasped. Wilson already crouched beside her, keeping his body between his daughter and the mess Brennan was making. However, it wasn't Kendra who'd been shot.

Sheridan lay bleeding in the snow.

"No," Rory whimpered as he crawled to Sheridan's side.

"Oh, love, no." Gripping Sheridan's hand, Rory brought it to his lips and kissed his palm. "Open yer eyes, Sheridan. Ye can't leave me now."

"Get your head out of your ass, man," Wilson barked, shrugging out of his jacket. "Put your coat under his head, then call it in. Your alpha-mate is a doctor, for god's sake."

Rory sucked in a harsh breath, then did as he'd been told. Wilson was right. He didn't have time to lose his shit. He needed to help his mate.

After Rory rolled up his coat and tucked it under Sheridan's head, he grabbed his phone from his pocket and dialed his alpha's number.

"Hello, Rory," Alpha Declan greeted. "How is yer mating going?"

"I have an emergency, Alpha," Rory cried as he watched Wilson press his own jacket against Sheridan's side. "Payne shot my mate, and Brennan killed him, and I need help."

"Where are ye?" the alpha immediately asked.

"The Caribou's parking lot."

"We're on our way. I'll have closer help to ye shortly," Declan assured. "Just hang on."

Rory didn't bother to reply. The sound of Sheridan's groan of pain cut through his heart like a knife. He hated he'd allowed his lover to get injured.

"Open yer eyes, Sheridan," Rory urged, holding his hand with one of his own while teasing his fingertips down his jaw. He knew Kendra held Sheridan's other hand while Wilson kept pressure on his wound. "Let me see those pretty hazel orbs."

"Ow," Sheridan muttered in a rough voice. "Damn, that hurts."

"My piggy bank is gonna be super full after this," Kendra stated, drawing a snort from Wilson.

Rory couldn't help but smile, too.

Peeling open his eyelids, Sheridan stared at him with an unfocused gaze. "Hi."

"Hi, my love," Rory murmured back. "You just rest. We're gonna get ye all healed up."

Sheridan hummed as he nodded just a little.

"Thank you," Wilson rumbled, his voice thick. "For jumping in front of Kendra. I" — his eyes teared — "can never make it up to you."

Smiling faintly, Sheridan murmured, "You don't have to make it up to me. We're family."

Wilson swallowed hard as he nodded. "Yeah. Yeah, we are."

"Hi, guys," a new voice greeted. "Heard you needed a hand."

Rory looked up and spotted a number of shifters heading their way. Seeing Doctor Ailean Carmichael hurrying over right next to Detective Grady Stryker, relief flooded him. The black jaguar shifter would help Sheridan while the tiger shifter could clear the scene.

Within five minutes, Rory's world righted itself. While the doctor shifter cleaned and stitched the wound, he confirmed that Sheridan would be just fine soon enough. The gunshot went through his side, but missed any vital organs. It was the force of his head hitting the frozen ground that had knocked him out.

Brennan showed up in a pair of sweats and a sweatshirt, his feet shoved back in his boots. He held Wilson and Kendra as he offered his heartfelt thanks to a slightly woozy Sheridan. His mate gave Brennan the same response he'd given Wilson.

"We're family."

As everyone nodded, Rory realized that never had truer words ever been spoken.

YOU MAY ALSO ENJOY THE FOLLOWING FROM EXTASY BOOKS INC:

Croc on the Menu
Charlie Richards

Excerpt

"Why the fuck aren't they answering their phones?"

Tideus Solverman snarled under his breath as he pressed harder on the accelerator. Weaving in and out of traffic, he ignored the speed limit, praying he wouldn't pick up a cop . . . or his motorcycle's tires wouldn't slip on the rain-slicked roads. He needed to get to the pub . . . ten minutes ago.

If the information Tideus had been sent was accurate, rogue shifters were going to kidnap Shifter Councilman Vincentius Goldstein while he enjoyed dinner at an Irish-themed pub that evening. Somehow, an ex-enforcer had found out about the reservation.

Note to self, tell the councilman never to make reservations in his name again.

Tideus worked as a council enforcer himself, and he couldn't understand how the half a dozen ex-enforcer shifters had justified going rogue. A pair of shifters who'd been council-members had been found guilty of crimes against their kind. Instead of enforcing the remaining council-members' decision to keep them under house arrest while they figured out the extent of their activities, six shifters had helped them flee.

It seemed now their numbers were growing. Those shifters that were egotistical, believing their race was superior to humans and shouldn't mate with them, saying Fate would never pair a shifter with someone so inferior. Other shifters who sided with them claimed the same about Fate and same-sex pairings.

Tideus thought they were all idiots. There was more than enough evidence to prove that Fate paired people based on who they needed in their life. A mate was a gift from the gods, a blessing, regardless of whether the person was man, woman, human, or paranormal.

I can't wait to find my mate. I'm gonna take ever-so-good care of him or her.

Having been with both sexes over the course of his centuries long life, Tideus couldn't give a shit what sex his mate turned out to be. Hell, he would accept an old man or woman and do his best to make their lives as amazing as possible even at an advanced age.

Tideus knew it helped that as soon as a human bonded with a paranormal, their aging practically screeched to a halt. The person would also gain increased health and vitality. Their bones would be harder to break, and their libido would skyrocket.

His crocodile rumbled in the back of his mind, making Tideus smile. "You and me both, buddy." At over two and a half centuries in age, he was beginning to lose patience.

When the Irish pub came into view — The Dancing Leprechaun — Tideus returned his focus to what he was doing. He veered into the parking lot, ignoring the honk of a car he'd cut off in the process. Tideus came to a stop in the slashed section at the end of the parking aisle and jumped from his motorcycle, whipping his helmet off in the process. Hearing the headgear hit the ground, Tideus knew he'd be sorry about that . . .

but later.

Shoving his keys into his pocket, Tideus jogged across the parking lot. He yanked open the door and rushed through. After a quick scan of the interior, he spotted the councilman, his mate, and his pair of guards at a table.

Tideus also noticed the four big men who'd just risen from a nearby table. One of them was an ex-enforcer named Richard. He'd retired almost two decades before, but Tideus knew his views had often mirrored those of the disgraced ex-councilmen's. Not surprising that they would have reached out to the black bear shifter.

Guess they're running a few minutes behind.

Never would Tideus be so grateful for whatever had delayed them. According to the information that a fellow enforcer had sent him—a spy by the name of Nkosi who was hidden within the bad guys' ranks—the shifters intended to take the councilman when he was twenty minutes into his meal. His reservation had been at seven, and right then, it was seven-thirty.

As Tideus started forward, a young woman stepped into his path. "Sir? Can I help you? Table for one?"

Tideus paused and leveled his look on the human, and she took a step backward as she held the menu to her chest as if it was a shield. Knowing what he looked like, he couldn't fault her for her unease. His skin a deep chocolate color and standing six-foot-five with broad shoulders and a heavily muscled frame, along with the fact that he wore torn jeans and a motorcycle jacket and boots, Tideus cut an intimidating figure.

"No, I'm here to see a friend," Tideus stated before brushing past her. He had just rounded the corner, leaving him five tables away from the councilman, when a pleasant aroma tickled his senses. Whipping his head around, Tideus paused, his mouth watering.

Once again, his crocodile rumbled in his mind.

Tideus met the deep brown eyes of a much shorter man, maybe standing five-foot-ten. The man hesitated an instant, then continued toward him. His expression firmed as he straightened his shoulders.

From the apron he wore, Tideus figured he worked there, maybe a manager. Considering his slight paunch, he might indulge in a little too much of his own product. Either that or he stood in one place for a lot of his day.

Without the green bandana around his head, Tideus thought his black curls would flop over his face. He found himself wondering how soft the man's hair was. His fingertips even twitched with his desire. Tideus could brush it away from his forehead as he nibbled along his slightly stubbled jaw.

What would this man taste like?

"Please, sir. Please, doona cause trouble here."

The stranger's softly spoken urging, coupled with his beautiful, lilting Irish accent, yanked Tideus out of his thoughts. It also made his balls tingle. Damn! He couldn't remember the last time he'd gotten so distracted by a handsome face . . . and this guy wasn't even what someone would call classically handsome. Instead, he was cute in that boy-next-door kind of way.

As Tideus took in a breath so he could reply, the human's scent tickled his senses again, more intensely.

Mate!

Tideus nearly gaped as his crocodile whispered in his mind.

Well, holy shit!

ABOUT THE AUTHOR

Charlie started writing fantasy when she was eight, and after stumbling onto her first erotic romance at age nineteen, she realized her true calling. She now focuses on writing gay erotic romance, normally of the paranormal variety, with heroes of all kinds. With the help and support of her husband, Charlie finally fulfilled one of her life-long goals . . . move to acreage with her horses. You can often find her curled up with her laptop and a cup of tea or glass of wine, creating her next adventure. Charlie enjoys exploring the mountains of her new Oregon home on horseback, 4-wheeler, or motorcycle.

She can be reached at ch.richards2010@yahoo.com
Or visit her at www.charlie-richards.com

www.ingramcontent.com/pod-product-compliance
Lightning Source LLC
Chambersburg PA
CBHW060646130626
46555CB00002B/984